"You'd do any type work? No limitations?" Greg Fields's navy blue eyes were guileless. "How about being a mistress?"

Stacy swallowed hard and stared at him. She had been propositioned before, but not from someone from whom she so desperately needed help.

"To whom?" she asked, wishing she could smack him one across his smug face.

"Well, if I'm to supply your needs, then I should be the one who gets satisfaction, don't you think?"

His free hand slid from her arm to her waist, using his fingers to hook into her belt, forcing her up off her feet so she had no way to brace away from him. His mouth touched hers, and the tremor from Stacy's body brought a moan from Greg.

"Don't tell me to stop, Stacy, because you know I can't. Once you make your mind up, there will be no turning back...."

Dear Reader,

It is our pleasure to bring you a new experience in reading that goes beyond category writing. The settings of **Harlequin American Romances** give a sense of place and culture that is uniquely American, and the characters are warm and believable. The stories are of "today" and have been chosen to give variety within the vast scope of romance fiction.

Against the backdrop of Arizona, Alaska, and Hawaii, Zelma Orr weaves a wonderful romance between a nurse and an architect that will whet your appetite to experience the beauty of these states.

From the early days of Harlequin, our primary concern has been to bring you novels of the highest quality. **Harlequin American Romances** are no exception. Enjoy!

Vivian Stephens

Vivian Stephens
Editorial Director
Harlequin American Romances
919 Third Avenue,
New York, N.Y. 10022

Miracles Take Longer

ZELMA ORR

Harlequin Books

TORONTO • NEW YORK • LOS ANGELES • LONDON
AMSTERDAM • PARIS • SYDNEY • HAMBURG
STOCKHOLM • ATHENS • TOKYO • MILAN

Published May 1983

First printing March 1983
Second printing March 1983
Third printing August 1983

ISBN 0-373-16007-0

Copyright © 1983 by Zelma Orr. All rights reserved.
Philippine copyright 1983. Australian copyright 1983.
Except for use in any review, the reproduction or utilization of
this work in whole or in part in any form by any electronic,
mechanical or other means, now known or hereafter invented,
including xerography, photocopying and recording, or in any
information storage or retrieval system, is forbidden without
the permission of the publisher, Harlequin Enterprises Limited,
225 Duncan Mill Road, Don Mills, Ontario, Canada M3B 3K9.

All the characters in this book have no existence outside the
imagination of the author and have no relation whatsoever to
anyone bearing the same name or names. They are not even
distantly inspired by any individual known or unknown to the
author, and all the incidents are pure invention.

The Harlequin trademarks, consisting of the words
HARLEQUIN AMERICAN ROMANCE and the portrayal
of a Harlequin, are trademarks of Harlequin Enterprises
Limited; the portrayal of a Harlequin is registered in the
United States Patent and Trademark Office and in the
Canada Trade Marks Office.

Printed in U.S.A.

Chapter One

The Pan American bus hissed to a stop a few yards in front of her, and Stacy trotted toward it, swinging agilely aboard.

"How much to the city?" she asked the big, good-natured-looking driver.

"Uptown or downtown?"

Stacy shrugged. "The westside, wherever that is."

"Eighty cents."

Conscious of the stares from the other passengers, Stacy dug into her jeans and counted the change into his hand, then moved back and found a seat near a window. She was thankful for the coolness of the air conditioning after her ride on Waco, her pony, who had been left at a small ranch. Looking up, she met the grinning stare of a bearded cowboy and returned his look for a moment, twisting in her seat to watch the countryside change from suburbs to the city. For a moment panic crowded into her throat and her stomach lurched.

She should have brought something to eat, she thought. She had left the reservation at four that morning, and it was now close to ten. Maybe after the call she could stop somewhere and splurge on a good breakfast. And feel guilty. She bit her lip.

"Young lady, next stop is Ranger Avenue, West. That close enough?" The driver was watching her in the mirror.

"That's fine," Stacy told him as she moved toward the front of the bus. Curious, appraising stares watched the almost bony figure make its way to the front of the bus. The jeans were not new, and though they were clean when she started out, they were now dusty and sweat-stained from hours of hard riding on her sorrel pony. Small built, barely five foot three inches and one hundred pounds, Stacy would be the first to admit she wasn't much to look at. Her most arresting features, bright jade-green eyes, were shadowed by thick, curved bangs. The dark hair, wound around her head in a thick braid, offered no softness to the tanned skin. Pale red lipstick, her only semblance of makeup, was for protection of her mouth against the hot, dry sun. Braided hair was the easiest to care for when you had neither time nor money for weekly beauty shop treatments.

Her informal mode of transportation by pony and bus was all she had, and the dusty jeans would have to be accepted. She had been away from the mainstream of life too long to know or care what styles were currently the rage.

She found a telephone booth not far from where she left the bus, and propped herself up to thumb through the Yellow Pages. Her eyes followed her finger down the page until she found the name she

Miracles Take Longer 9

wanted and, repeating the address to herself, walked down Ranger Avenue. It was not the thickest part of the business district, but it was quiet and neat-looking, towering graystone buildings making up the bulk of the section.

Boring into her mind was the contrast of Ranger Avenue on Phoenix's westside to the reservation she had left behind early that morning. The streets were clean, no tumbleweeds or sand flying ahead of constant twenty-miles-per-hour winds. In the midmorning sunlight the buildings might have recently been whitewashed, so free of dust they were, rising from the ground in a symmetric design that could have been furnished only by an experienced architect bent on putting the biggest buildings on the least amount of real estate. Like Greg Fields—her target for today.

As if that thought gave rise to her destination, the Broderick Building loomed in front of her, a forbidding structure that took her breath.

"Jeepers," she mumbled to herself as she gazed upward. "Looks like they'd scale these things down so as not to overshadow the entire human race."

Climbing thirty-five stories into the clear desert air, the glass-fronted building dominated its smaller neighbors. Glare-proof windows, reflecting heat and light away from the inside, reminded Stacy of unseeing eyes unable to focus on any target. Blind, like people who refused to see. Her lips tightened and she straightened her shoulders, took a deep breath, and walked through the wide doors that opened automatically as she thrust out her hand to push.

Of course, she thought, *I should have known the mar-*

vels of the electronic age are everywhereß except at the Mati Reservation.

By the elevator she checked the names, then waited for the next car going to the fifteenth floor. When the doors slid back, Stacy stepped out and walked the rich carpeted hallway to the receptionist's desk.

The woman sitting at the desk was beautiful, from the top of her blond head, to her midriff, which was as far as Stacy could see. There was no way she could tell if the honey-colored hair came from a bottle, but the eyelashes had to be false—at least an inch long, and black, framing eyes of dark brown. Lips in a perfect cupid's bow of coral pursed into a question as she glanced up and saw Stacy, pausing in her cosmetic repairs long enough to say, "Yes?"

"I'd like to see Mr. Fields, please," Stacy told her.

The wide eyes behind the incredible lashes moved over the nondescript figure standing before her and dismissed it as unimportant. "Do you have an appointment?"

"No."

"Oh, I'm afraid he won't be able to see you, then. I can set you up with an appointment for three o'clock Friday afternoon." The blonde's smile was cool, meant to get rid of unwanted pests.

Stacy bit her lip. "I'm from out of town and won't be here Friday. It's important I see him now."

The lovely blonde stood up, stretched to show off a more than adequate figure, and walked across the deep beige carpet to the water cooler. "I'm sorry, miss." The smile was calculated to tell her how sorry she really was. But it was lost on Stacy. She had long since learned that to ignore ill-mannered people was easier than getting your blood pressure up. She watched Miss Blonde wiggle her way across the room, turned and moved down the hallway. The door with the gold-lettered name of Greg Fields, Architect, was open, and she walked through as though she knew where she was going.

A cool voice questioned her. "Can I help you, miss?" And Stacy turned to see another movie-star beautiful, statuesque blonde looking her over. Didn't they have anything but beauty queens working in these places? she thought, conscious of her own appearance.

"Yes. I'm looking for Mr. Fields," she responded.

"May I ask who is calling?" Well, at least her manners were better, Stacy thought.

"I'm Stacy Waring from the Mati River Indian Reservation. I don't have an appointment, but it is important that I see Mr. Fields." She braced herself for the inevitable.

The blonde frowned. "I'm sorry, Miss Waring, I'm afraid Mr. Fields can't see you without an appointment."

Stacy took a deep breath, but before she could protest, the inner door to another office swung open and a tall figure plowed through the room to the desk.

"Look, Greta, I need these prints over at the site right away. Call Stubbs and see if he has someone who can pick them up." Greta moved to lift the phone and dial even before he had finished speaking, and thus ignored, Stacy followed the man she guessed to be Mr. Fields as he headed back into his own inner sanctum.

He shoved the door behind him, but Stacy's outstretched hand caught it and she eased herself into the room before pushing the door closed.

"Mr. Fields?" He swung around and stared. She waited as his eyes went from head to foot and back again, waited patiently until the soot-rimmed navy blue eyes met her own green ones.

His investigation of her complete, he asked, "May I help you?"

"You certainly can." Stacy let out a breath of relief and grinned.

Still standing, watching her, he motioned her to a chair. She sat down, realizing for the first time that she was tired. He dropped into the chair behind his desk and waited for her to begin.

Leaning forward, she told him, "The only way I know how to begin is with a very flat statement. I'm from the Mati River Indian Reservation and I need help."

As she hestitated, he said, "And where do I fit in, Miss...?"

"I'm sorry. I'm Stacy Waring." She plunged on. "Mr. Fields, I need medicine for my people on the reservation. If I can get antibiotics, first-aid kits, and syringes, I will have enough to work with for a while. At least more than I have now."

"Your people, Miss Waring? You're not an Indian."

"No. I'm a VISTA representative."

"I see." He studied her. "Am I right, Miss Waring, in that VISTA provides the settlement where you work with medical supplies as well as a doctor?"

She was surprised at his knowledge of the organization. Very few people knew or cared what was or was not provided. She stared at the floor, reluctant to reveal her reasons for such a demand.

"Yes, those things are provided. But it doesn't mean that the people who need it get it."

"What is that supposed to mean?" She was a bit uncomfortable under his appraising stare.

"We still need the basic medical supplies, and since I'm a registered nurse, I can take care of most of their needs unless it's an emergency."

"Who is the doctor assigned?"

"A Dr. Grove, from Flagstaff." She opened her mouth to add more, but thought better of it.

"Dr. Grove is a well-known physician. I'm sure he does everything he can do for your people." Greg Fields's dark blue eyes stayed on her as his left hand reached for a pipe resting in a holder on the corner of the slate-topped desk. A tanned hand, with strong, slim fingers, not soft looking as she would have thought. No rings or evidence of any having been worn. Unmarried. No, these days, men seldom wore a wedding band. Or did they? She had no knowledge in that area at all. Her glance followed his movements as he struck a wooden match on the emery board side of a small box. It was an unstudied move, one he was accustomed to making, taking his time experiencing pleasure from this indulgence.

His evaluation of Dr. Grove was so different from her own that she couldn't keep the resentment from showing in her voice. "Dr. Grove is a selfish, grasping, uncaring disgrace to the medical profession,"

Stacy told him through clenched teeth. "He gives us the barest necessities, sometimes not even that, and covers himself so no one knows what's going on. He is the classic example of the greedy government-connected bigwig who is getting rich off the misery of the little people. We could drown him in the river and never miss him. Ask the people who wait for the little dole he gives them. Better still, ask me. Better than that, go with me and let me show you." She was breathing hard as she was reminded of all the inequities in the system she helped support.

At the beginning of her outburst Greg Fields had leaned forward, elbows on his desk, and had not taken his eyes from her face. Now he asked, "Why haven't you reported him to someone who can change things? The object should be to rid him of any authority and replace him with someone who is interested in the people."

Stacy smiled. "If you care to look over some of my papers, Mr. Fields, I can show you a stack of correspondence that you wouldn't believe, trying to get someone to listen to me. No one wants to admit we have crooks in this game, but believe me, we have some of the worst. Replace him? I'm not a dreamer any longer, Mr. Fields. I need a miracle, but miracles take longer, and I don't have the time." She shrugged. "It is a thankless job, I can't deny that, and I don't blame anyone for not wanting it, but I do blame them for taking what rightfully belongs to the Indians."

There was a long silence as they stared at each other. No wonder he wanted beautiful girls around,

Stacy thought; he was quite lovely himself. Not too apt a description for the man who sat opposite her at the desk, perhaps. Black hair, almost a crew cut, but with a slight curl he must try hard to subdue. The indentation in his chin, only the suggestion of a dimple, could easily be an invitation for inquiring fingers—or lips. He either spent a lot of time out of doors or under a sun lamp in some plush athletic club to have skin that smooth shade of bronze. She opted for the club, thinking he probably spent more time satisfying the female population's physical desires than he did out in the sun. With those eyes, so dark a blue you'd have to identify them as navy, and short, thick lashes providing a pleasing frame for them, he could charm the very coolest of the species. Strong, broad shoulders that would be excellent for crying purposes, and all she wanted from him was money.

His physical appearance certainly complemented the office with its simply understated, expensive furnishings. From the wine leather executive chair behind the six-foot-wide solid oak desk, to the heavy cream damask draperies drawn over the sun-dappled windows, to the deep plushness of matching carpet, no cost had been spared to give an overall picture of success. Stacy admitted to being impressed, knowing too that her opinion didn't count for much.

Odd how she had picked Greg Fields to call on for her first outbreak against the unjust situation she couldn't handle alone. Going through the paper she received in her mail, she spotted his picture at some groundbreaking ceremony. Reading about the skyrocketing popularity of the young architect, she caught the glimmer of an idea. Looking back, she decided she must have been on the fringe of lunacy to invade his private office to ask him outright for money. Maybe he was trading on his popularity and had no assets over and above that. She shook her head, not yet despairing of convincing him she was sincere in the need for medical supplies.

"Am I to assume that you want me to replace some of the money Dr. Grove is, uh, using for other than the purpose intended?" He squinted at her through the thin pipe smoke.

"Not replace, Mr. Fields. I don't want money. Get me the supplies. I'll give you a list of what I need most. I can prove the need, show you who needs it. If you think I find it easy to beg, I don't. I've been on the reservation for ten months, trying any and every legal way, anything that I thought would help, and you're my last resort."

"Very commendable, Miss Waring." She detected a slight mocking tone in his voice, and her body stiffened. "So you want me to donate several hundred dollars toward your pet project. I'll bet with your sweet, innocent look you get what you want too."

As a rule, Stacy was slow to anger, giving people the benefit of any doubt, but this was a problem she had lived with for so long, fought for solutions, used up most of her savings for, and she wasn't about to admit defeat. Not even his sarcasm would make her back down—not yet.

"Mr. Fields," she said his name slowly to quiet her rapid breathing, "my year with VISTA will be up at the end of September. As an architect, you can use an errand runner, odd-job performer, or whatever. I'm a college graduate, a registered nurse. I'll work for no pay to cover the supplies I want from you now. You have the contacts, people you know will donate as much as I need and it won't even interrupt their briefest cocktail hour."

As she stopped, he leaned back in his chair and whistled. "You really are serious, aren't you?" His probing blue eyes made her squirm. He was silent so long she wondered if he had forgotten she was there. With absentminded movements he tapped the pipe against the ashtray, emptying the tobacco from it. Finally he asked, "You'd do any type work? No limitations?"

She smiled at him. "I wouldn't like to commit murder unless you double the amount."

The navy blue eyes were guileless as he asked, "How about being a mistress, say, for three months?"

Stacy swallowed hard and stared. She had been propositioned before, but not by someone from whom she was begging. Her life had not been thoroughly sheltered, and she had seen the seamy side more than any other. He could be baiting her, waiting for her to throw in the towel.

"To whom?" she asked, watching his easy smile and wishing she could smack him one across his self-satisfied face.

"Well, if I'm to supply your needs, then I should be the one who gets satisfaction, don't you think?"

"Are you serious?" She leaned forward a little, frowning.

He nodded. "Very."

She thought to herself, *All those gorgeous blondes he has around him and he'd take me? Nonsense.*

His eyebrows raised, Mr. Fields said, "Well?"

"Do I get a chance to think it over, or do you want the answer before I collect my supplies?" She was beginning to like the way his eyebrows went up to ask questions before his voice did.

"I'm a businessman, Miss Waring. I want my answer first." He stood up, eyes going once more over Stacy's erect figure, from the dark heavy braids to her dusty boots. He walked to the window, pushed the drapes to one side, staring down at the sidewalk, giving her a chance to examine him without appearing to stare.

Greg Fields wasn't much more than thirty years old, she guessed. Must be well over six feet, and slim, with narrow hips. The light gray suit he wore flexed with his movements, giving credence to her belief it was tailored to his exact measurements and cost more than she made in a year with VISTA. One hand casually pushed the suit jacket back and rested on his hip, showing a pale blue shirt and darker tie that matched his eyes. Stacy knew he walked over there so she could observe all that masculinity, and he had succeeded too, because he was worth watching.

"Have you had lunch? You could make your decision over a drink, maybe?"

I haven't even had breakfast, she wanted to tell him, but instead, she shook her head. "No, no lunch yet. I'll get something later." She could picture herself walking into a fancy restaurant, such as he frequented, in her dusty blue jeans. Even she was not that brave, she conceded.

"We'll eat lunch now," he said, turning to the desk and picking up the telephone.

"Mr. Fields, surely you can see that I'm not dressed for lunch in the places you go," she said somewhat sharply.

He hesitated and looked her over as if just noticing she wasn't dressed in suitable clothing for anything "Okay. We'll go to my place. I won't argue over what you have on."

She stiffened. "I'd rather not."

"Afraid? Listen, anyone who'll barge into a strange man's office with the request you just came up with shouldn't be afraid to have lunch at his apartment." A mocking smile played over the firm lips.

"I'm not afraid." Stacy thought of Allie and Dade back on the reservation. If she had a fancy meal, it would be the first one in ten months, and all she could think of was her friends getting just enough food to keep them from being too weak to walk around. Her lips tightened.

"All right, Mr. Fields. I'm hungry. Let's go." She stood up.

"Good girl." He grinned. "And the name's Greg." Together they left the office.

"Greta, I'll be at home for the next couple of hours. Refer any important calls to me there." He ignored the curious look directed at Stacy.

"Yes, sir." Greta was much too poised to let him know what she was thinking.

The light blue car they entered in the underground

garage was new by Stacy's standards, but she paid little attention to cars, saw very few in her everyday life, and didn't recognize the model. They drove through late noon traffic, and about fifteen minutes later, turned into a drive beneath a luxury apartment building, and a man was there waiting to park for him. They took the elevator up to the top floor, six stories up.

The apartment was plush, as Stacy had expected. The room they entered was big enough to dwarf even Greg Fields's bigger-than-life frame, and Stacy hesitated just inside the door, eyes narrowed, jolted by the stark contrast of her life and this man's, about which she knew nothing. Except that he had money, some of which she hoped to get if she had to beg or borrow. Not steal. She couldn't go that far, even for the Mati.

The carpet beneath her dusty boots was a deep rust, thick enough to remind her of walking in the deep sand of the desert. Pictures of southwestern art decorated two walls. Above the oversize couch was a painting of mountains stretching into the distance, a simmering desert with a rutted trail across it, four horses pulling a Wells Fargo stage at breakneck speed, indicated by the swirling dust. On the opposite wall hung an original painting by C.M. Russell, recognizable even to Stacy by the signature over the outline of a steer skull, depicting the roundup of cattle, the movement of the cowboys on their horses as one action. With a slight shake of her head at what the painting must have set him back, she let her eyes wander around the furnishings.

The beige leather couch was placed behind a glass-topped cocktail table, and two leather club chairs of a shade darker material were angled to face the couch. Greg had walked ahead of her to a hidden bar that appeared behind what looked to Stacy's untrained eyes to be glass doors. He turned to look at her, his back to the heavy draperies that exactly matched the carpet.

"What do you drink?" He smiled at her, eyes taking in her figure that was standing almost at attention.

"Nothing."

His straight-lined eyebrows went up. "Nothing?"

"Nothing," she repeated, without apology.

He watched her for a moment, pushed the glasses he held to one side, and picked up the phone. After a brief pause he said, "This is Greg Fields. Send up two sliced chicken sandwiches and two iced teas. Yes, thanks."

He turned toward her, and said, "Now Miss Waring. Stacy, is it?"

"That's it." She crossed the room to one of the chairs. Good thing it was leather, she thought, as dusty as she was. He waited until she sat down, then sprawled on the couch.

She looked up to find him studying her. He grinned. "You are a puzzle, Stacy. I find you hard to believe."

"In what way, Mr. Fields?" she asked him, all but holding her breath.

"Greg," he corrected her. "Well, in the first place, I know Dr. Grove pretty well. It never occurred to me that he would ever try to do anyone out of what was rightfully his. By well, I mean we've played golf, we're members of a couple of the same clubs, and he's on the Board of Architects out of Flagstaff and Phoenix. I see him at these places sometimes. He doesn't strike me as a thief."

"Mr. Fields—"

"Greg."

"You aren't taking me seriously, are you?" Stacy stood up, walking away from her chair, ramrod stiff. Determined to get an answer from him, preferably a positive one, she forced herself to go back and face him. For a moment she wondered what the representatives of VISTA would say if they knew what she was doing, and that in itself made up her mind to go on with what she'd started. VISTA gave you the problems and said solve them, no matter how.

She was conscious of him watching her, smiling at her discomfort. "Look, granted I went about this all wrong. Granted I got the wrong man when out of all the people in the Yellow Pages, I pick someone who thinks Dr. Grove is a nice guy. I'm not being facetious when I say I want nothing for myself. Those people on that reservation haven't got the basic necessities, much less anything extra. I want to be able to give the children all their shots, penicillin for colds, even aspirin." She paused.

"How much money does VISTA pay you?" Greg inquired.

She stiffened. "I don't see—"

"How much?" he persisted.

She pressed her lips together, frowning.

"Stacy?"

"Monthly pay is fifty-seven dollars, plus room and board."

The brows climbed. "What do you do with that bankroll?" he asked in a sarcastic tone. "Room and board? What exactly does that consist of?"

A knock on the door kept her from answering. It was their lunch. When the table was set by a young man in a spotless white coat, Stacy wondered what had happened to the plain old chicken sandwich. It was a small banquet spread out on the oak dinette table in the little alcove off the living room. She realized she was hungry enough to be weak.

Greg walked behind her, waited for her to sit down, and eased her chair up to the table. "As you were saying, you spend all that money how?"

Stacy shrugged, busy with her food. "On necessities."

"Yours?"

"If I have any," she admitted, wishing for a change of subject.

"What do you consider a necessity, Stacy?"

She put down her fork, dropped her hands to her lap, and asked, "What are you after, Mr. Fields?"

"Greg," he corrected. "Just information. I have to know about any enterprise I plan to invest in."

A dart of hope spread through her. Leaning forward, she asked, "Do you want to hear the story of my life, or do you want to hear the story of the Mati River Reservation?"

"I want to hear the story of your life—and how you became involved in the Mati River Reservation."

Aware that she had been stalling, she tried one

more tactic. "You told Greta you'd be gone a couple of hours. If you listen to this tale of woe, it will be much longer."

He smiled. "I have lots of time, and Greta is a great secretary. She'll call if she needs to get in touch with me."

Chapter Two

The circumstances under which Stacy Waring was born were anything but glamorous. Her mother wasn't living with any of her numerous husbands when Stacy came along, and it was doubtful if she really knew which one was the father of this unwanted bundle of dark, squalling humanity. It was a last touch of romantic idealism that made her hang the unlikely name of Stacy on such a plain infant. Soon after Stacy's birth, her mother placed her on the courthouse steps and disappeared.

So began a series of foster homes, each one caring less as the child grew older. It meant a few extra dollars and an extra pair of hands to work. The one good thing that came out of being assigned to foster homes was the requirement that she attend school until she was at least sixteen. A willing student, Stacy hated it when she was kept home from school on some pretense, but usually for running errands or doing housework. When foster children care became the responsiblity of the Welfare Board of the state, regular attendance at school was a must, and reports of that attendance made on a monthly basis—all in Stacy's favor.

When she was seventeen, she moved out of the latest home to which she had been assigned, took a cheap efficiency room, and never went back. No one cared, nor checked to see if she was all right.

Nights, holidays, Saturdays, and Sundays, Stacy worked as a waitress, saving pennies, dimes, and nickels. She ate barely enough, except when the diner fed her, and ignored the natural hunger for extras that all teen-agers experience. Forced by lifelong circumstances to be a rigid economist, she found it easy to resist extras such as new dresses and hair treatments. She bought an ancient treadle sewing machine for a hard-earned fifteen dollars and made her own clothing and curtains for her bare and drafty living room windows.

At her high school graduation she received her diploma with no one there to be proud of her better-than-average grades. She started college, working toward her degree as a registered nurse, aided by a state scholarship and her savings from her job.

Stacy had few dates, and sometimes an unknown longing pulled at her, and she termed these days as her "boy blue days," but whatever it was that she was missing would have to wait.

In less than three years she earned her Bachelor of Science in nursing, taking summer courses and heavy schedules, reducing the normal four-year term by a substantial amount. During her last year she trained at a Veterans Administration hospital and dated one of the young interns there. The night he parked on the riverbank and she had to fight her way out of the car and walk eight miles home had been the end of that romance. It wasn't difficult for her to forget about dating and concentrate on her job.

For two years, her home was the huge General Hospital in Philadelphia. The cold gray building housed her friends and what amounted to all the family she had, and she felt lucky to have that much. Working double shifts and taking extra shifts for the popular nurses, she was able to pay back the money she borrowed to finish out her scholarship fund.

She was twenty-four years old the day she decided her "boy blues" were going to be permanent if she didn't make a change—a drastic one. She observed her female co-workers giggle and blink their long lashes at the new interns, even the patients, saw the men respond, and she wondered about herself and her inability to play up to the male species. The difference must be in the lack of family to fill out her life, to praise or criticize, to care. She couldn't make small talk over what to wear, what she'd have for dinner, a new formal for a dinner dance, or the new car she was planning to buy. She was busy surviving, a loner from birth, and lonely.

Her interest perked up when a special recruiting team came to Philadelphia General looking for recruits for the Volunteers in Service To America program, and Stacy picked up literature on her way to the dormitory one morning as she left the graveyard shift.

She showered and slipped into cotton pajamas, stretching out her tired body. The VISTA pamphlets lay on the lamp table, and she thumbed through them, reading a paragraph here and there. According to the information printed there, money was scarce and benefits few and far between in the VISTA program, but what they offered was the chance of feeling a deep sense of satisfaction in ministering to your needy fellow man, woman, and child.

Stacy smiled to herself. Few people were as needy as she herself had been many times in her life. The papers slipped from her hand, and she slept.

It was nearly a week later when Stacy went down to VISTA headquarters and applied to take the test for placement. *I must be nuts,* she decided, when she found out the exact amount of money she would be paid, and the conditions they would sometimes face as they lived in poor settlements. She was just beginning to command a decent salary as a nurse, and her savings at last came above a hundred dollars, with a promise of much better earnings a sure thing. Nevertheless, she signed the papers, and when asked what country she preferred to work in, she replied, "Mine."

Stacy would never forget her first sight of her home for the next year. The bus dropped her at a small mail station, three and a half miles from the Mati River Reservation, which was nestled in the semi-arid desert of Arizona, twenty miles northwest of Phoenix. As she approached the part adobe, part trash buildings that housed the one hundred residents of the reservation, she had a sudden desire to turn and run. Her high aspirations to help her countrymen came very close to evaporation as she gazed at the dismal excuse for living quarters.

Her brief instructions on the history of the small

tribe of Havasupai Indians who inhabited the canyon had not prepared her for the total primitive conditions in which they lived. Their one claim to fame was a small stream of crystal clear water that came from some unknown source. And that was the only running water between the reservation and Phoenix, the Mati.

The inhabitants of the reservation had the fight taken out of them years ago, caught between their desire to remain true to their Indian heritage and the power of the federal government to erode the small bit of land they claimed. They were stray descendants of a once-proud tribe, now reduced to fighting for survival by supplying transportation to the few visitors who came into their canyon, renting horses and mules to them. The weather was severely cold only a short few weeks during the worst of winter, but summers shimmered in blistering heat with only a few scrubs of mesquite bush and cottonwoods to shelter them.

Stacy was accepted as just another link in the chain of thorns the government inflicted on the people of the reservation in the name of "assistance." It took weeks to get them to even acknowledge that she was there; weeks of frustration in which she discovered how far from reality the VISTA program had drifted in that area.

Dade, whose name meant Father of All, was one of the higher ranking chiefs, and Stacy became well acquainted with him because his six-year-old daughter, Allie, an adorable outgoing bronzed-skin doll, became ill and they couldn't get a doctor out to the reservation. Dr. Grove, out of Flagstaff, was their medical representative, but according to all reports, was seldom seen. Looking around her, Stacy thought, *I'll bet he's seldom seen, and who can really blame him?*

Checking Allie's temperature, Stacy found it over one hundred and two degrees and, without hesitation, gave her baths from her slim supply of alcohol and, when the temperature failed to drop, used the penicillin tablets she had been saving. It took twenty-four hours of constant attention, but Allie recovered from the severe virus attack within three days. Dade's family became Stacy's steadfast support in the near-hostile reservation, and through his influence she was grudgingly accepted.

Most of the inhabitants of the reservation were old; very few of the younger people stayed if they could find anything else to do in the city, becoming migrant, going anywhere they could make a little money. The women who remained were too old for childbearing and Stacy was thankful for that, seeing no need to bring babies into such a luckless existence. They still wove baskets, using the complicated twined and coiled methods, selling them to stray tourists or archaeologists who stumbled into the blind canyon. The men hunted along the stream, and several miles beyond the canyon up the small waterway fish were still abundant. Stacy was amazed daily by the fact that anything stayed around in a country that fought humans every step of the way.

One of the young Indians who returned to the settlement after graduating from the University of Arizona was Star, the great grandson of a chief who fought the Americans every rough mile across the

Miracles Take Longer

west. Star was still fighting, and his open rebellion at the way his people were treated was a sore spot with his elders. He refused to accept the federal rules and regulations without something to show for them, and he had left a good teaching position to come back to his home to fight for whatever he could get for them. There was bitterness in the dark eyes as he fought the unyielding ignorance and acceptance of their stance in life by his people, and he was openly resentful of everything Stacy tried to do.

It was Stacy's nature to admire anyone who fought for what he thought was right, so she gave Star plenty of room to question the purpose of the classes she taught, lessons she tried to put across to the younger Indians. But she could take just so much of his taunting disbelief in her work. Star found this out one day as he sat insolently watching as she taught American history to a small class of eight-year-olds.

Before dismissing the class, Stacy said, "Would you stay for a moment after the children leave, Star? I have a question."

He was waiting for her in the back of the room as the children filed in orderly fashion through the side of the lean-to she used as a classroom. She waited until they had gone into the compound area, where they threw balls and raced each other for entertainment, then turned to Star as he unlimbered his long legs and waited. He was tall and thick shouldered, his jet-black hair down over his collar. The broad nose fit into the bronzed face through wide set dark eyes. The wide mouth, with thick lips, seldom showed any relaxation or attempt to smile, sternness stamped on his face permanently. She knew of his run-ins with Dade and his tribal chiefs, and though she could say nothing that would approve or disapprove of their laws, she found herself in agreement with him, but he never acknowledged the fact that she made an effort to help everyone.

Stacy went to meet Star as he stood and walked toward her, disdain for her and all she stood for evident in the movement of his body. As they stopped just a step apart, her right hand met his cheek with a resounding slap. The dark eyes narrowed and a muscle moved in the taut cheek, but he said nothing.

Stacy wasn't angry, she was mad clear through. "You listen to me, Star, and you listen good. I'm here because I asked to be here, and I believe in what I'm doing. Does that sound corny to you? It may or may not be as much as I can do, but for now it will have to suffice. I know your people are neglected, and have been for hundreds of years, but I didn't do it. And I'm trying to rectify some of the mistakes as best I can. I'm sure I'll make mistakes too, but it won't be in trying to injure you or your people. I need help too—your help. Now, would you mind telling me what you have against me, and never mind saying anything about the color of my skin."

The cold darkness of his eyes did not lessen as he studied the angry young woman in front of him. "The ways of the white man have not changed over the years. They still give with one hand and take back with both. You make a show of living as the Indian lives, but you can't wait to get back to your own civilization."

"This is my civilization. And you're right, I can

hardly wait to get away from the likes of you. Your kind is found in Indians, white, or mixed colors. It isn't pride you feel for your people, it's resentment that you aren't still lord of the land. I don't blame you, but don't you blame me either." By this time she was standing so that her uplifted face almost touched his chin, her hands on hips, her feet braced apart. Star felt the seething anger in the small body. Without seeming to move, his arms came down, encircling her waist, and pulled her against him. The dark head bent and his mouth covered hers for a brief moment. When he released her, he stepped back and braced for the expected blow. Instead, she stared for one instant, then turned her back on him and walked away, angry tears blurring her vision. She knew that his action had not been meant as romantic, but was his way of showing what he thought of a young white woman with the nerve to think she could change things he, as a native of the reservation, had not been able to do.

As she organized mixed games with the children later in the afternoon, Star joined them, never mentioning their conversation or the kiss, nor did she. Since that day, some six months before, he had never touched her. There had been many times when she caught his dark eyes broodingly following her, and he stayed close by, helping with the older children, sternly cautioning them about rough horseplay. Whether he believed in what she was doing was hard to tell since he talked little, but she let him know how appreciative she was in little ways, though he never acknowledged the fact.

Dr. Grove was Star's pet hatred. Before Stacy had time to find out about his underhanded healings,

Star's hostility made her wonder. The epidemic of flu among the older people, and measles among the young, opened her eyes. Little Allie caught every virus that came along and she kept a cold. Stacy watched her closely, suspecting that their food, consisting a lot of menus made strictly from corn meal, and lack of vitamins was the culprit.

When she asked about shots, Dade shook his head. "No shots."

"She must have had shots, Dade. On the books your section has had all the serum for vaccinations the children need. Especially gamma globulin for measles."

"No money for shots," Dade insisted stubbornly.

Stacy explained. "There's no charge, Dade. The shots are free and the Service wants you to have them because it's dangerous not to get them."

"Dr. Grove say no pay, no shots."

Stacy could feel her patience slipping. Dr. Grove was in Flagstaff and not due to drop by the small settlement for two more weeks. The serum should be at the Center.

When she left her small shack that served as her room and office that evening, Stacy went to the Medical Center, the adobe building that housed Dr. Grove's office and all his records—the only near-decent building on the reservation. To her surprise, the files were locked, and Rachel, one of the few young Indian girls left at home, who worked as Dr. Grove's clerk and errand girl, told her that he always locked them and took the keys with him.

Thoughtfully Stacy thanked her and left. The only information on file should be shots and a few medical facts about the people on the reservation and there was certainly nothing about them that she didn't know. As a registered nurse she had most likely done more for them than a doctor who seldom put in an appearance and was never there when needed.

What did he do with the medical supplies supposed to be within her reach for minor aches and ailments? A locked outside door would keep the honest inhabitants out of the building, and none of them had ever shown an interest in what was kept there. A lot of *why*'s and *what*'s kept circling in Stacy's head as she sought reasons why Allie and the other smaller children hadn't had the shots recommended. There were cases where people were shortchanged in their supplies, but the minimal amount that was provided for the few Havasupai who remained in the area wouldn't be worth stealing.

Dr. Grove did not return at the end of two weeks as he had said he would, and Stacy couldn't wait any longer, and embarked on her one-way crusade to get help for her friends.

Stacy looked up from the bread she was tearing into tiny pieces to find Greg's dark blue eyes watching her every move. She waited for him to speak.

When he finally spoke, it wasn't what she was expecting. "And you think you can change the centuries-old customs of the Indians to conform to your modern ideas in one short year, Stacy? I'm afraid you're far from realistic." He stood up. "They like the way they live, regardless if it's the best or as much as they could have. Most of them are too lazy—"

She was on her feet, shoving the chair back so that it rocked before it fell, making a soft thump on the thick carpet. Her hands clenched into fists, green eyes bright with anger, her small body tense as she faced him. "You don't know what you're talking about. What would you do with five acres of rock soil that won't grow a hill of beans, Mr. Fields? Oh, of course, you'd build a beautiful country club and five-hundred-thousand dollar condominiums. That's what the land's good for—growing cement."

Greg's hands went out to her, but she brushed them aside and turned to pick up the chair, conscious of being near tears, her hands shaking. Her voice was muffled as she said, "I'm sorry. I shouldn't take it out on you. All outsiders feel the same way, and that's the problem. No one knows what it's like to live as these people do, and, furthermore, don't want to be bothered about it."

Greg's hands on her shoulders turned her to face him, and he shook his head. "Such strong words from such a little girl." His eyes went to the heavy braids of hair, back to her still angry eyes. "Is it very hard to keep your hair like that? Is it all yours?"

She swallowed. "No. Yes." At his raised eyebrows she clarified, "No, it isn't hard to fix. Yes, it's all mine."

"How long is it?"

"To my waist."

He smiled. "That isn't far. There's not much of you." He took her hand, leading her to the couch, and when they were seated, continued to look at her hair.

"How does it come down?" His hand moved over the braids, searching for pins.

Stacy caught his hand, laughed at him as she removed two large strategically located pins, and unwrapped the braids from around her head, letting them fall in front of her shoulders.

"Beautiful. Someday soon, I'd like to see it unbraided," he whispered as he tilted her chin and kissed her lips lightly, his hand playing with one braid just over the curve of her breast.

Stacy stiffened and was about to lash out at him when she remembered their half-decided deal. She watched the concentration on his face as he continued to caress the thick braid. He closed his fingers around it, pulling her closer to him, his mouth skimming her cheeks, along the curve to her throat, to the hollow just above the opening of her cotton shirt. One hand cupped the back of her head as he returned to her mouth, tasting, enjoying the flavor, increasing the pressure until she felt her reserve slipping and her lips parted. Long, black lashes settled against her tanned cheek, and she sighed as her hands came up under his arms to hold him close.

Her fingers probing into his rib cage, Stacy moved against him, feeling the thud of his heartbeat against the roundness of her breasts. He let go of the braid, his free hand moving from her waist around her back, fingers spreading over her hip, down to her thigh. In one last effort Stacy moved away from him, pushing at his chest as she brought her hands forward, but he showed no signs of releasing her, until she moaned, twisting her body.

His hold loosened on her, but he continued to look down into her face, studying the questioning look in the green eyes. One finger came up to trace her lips, over the line of her jaw, to the pulse beating below it.

His voice was quiet as he asked, "And what about our bargain, Stacy? What kind of terms can we agree on?"

"Do we have a bargain?" she asked, hope building inside her.

"I can hold up my part of it," he told her, smiling down into her face.

She took a deep breath, pulling away from him, finding it difficult to think or breathe while he was holding her against his chest where she could feel the beat of his heart. It was taking some getting used to, having a man like Greg Fields bargain with her in a way that she had never thought about, much less planned for. She had vowed to do anything it took to get help for the Mati residents, but this was not exactly what she had in mind.

"I don't know how these things are handled," she told him, "but I need a thousand dollars, and I need it tomorrow." She may as well push her luck and get it while he was willing—for the price he mentioned.

"What kind of guarantee do I have that I can collect on the loan?"

She hesitated. "A promissory note?" She swallowed. "You know I'm not going anywhere, so you won't have trouble finding me to collect. Do you want me to sign some papers?"

He smiled, and shook his head. "Since we're dealing with Indians, maybe I should make us blood brothers and sisters to insure my pay."

Anger sparked in her eyes, and she stood up. "Stop making fun of me. If I get the money, I'll repay you one way or another. I'd rather work for you, but—" Her hand made an uncertain gesture. "If you're sure you want an extra girl friend for three months, I'll agree to that."

He watched her agitated movements. "Where are you staying tonight?"

"You skip subjects so often, I never know where you'll be next."

"You're keeping up. Where?"

She shrugged. "I was going back to the reservation, but since I have to stay over for the money, I'm sure I can find someplace nearby."

"You can stay here."

She smiled at him. "I'm a businesswoman, Mr. Fields. No money, no deal."

"I'll stay somewhere else." He sat up straight. "How much money do you have?"

She felt the blush spread over her face and throat. "Enough." Some fast calculating told her she wouldn't have enough to eat and take the bus back down the highway fifteen miles, but she could sleep at the bus station. Her mind was busy planning ahead.

"Stay here, and I'll drive you to the reservation tomorrow after we get your money and some supplies."

"I left Waco—my horse—at a ranch about fifteen miles outside of town. I'll have to pick him up."

"I'll take care of that." He frowned. "At the Alto Ranch?"

"Yes. How did you know?" This Greg Fields was going to be a man to reckon with. *Am I capable?* she wondered. *I have no choice,* she decided.

He grinned. "The only one between here and the reservation, so I guessed."

He crossed the room to the phone and dialed. He talked to Greta, then made two more calls in rapid succession, evidently getting the answers he sought. *Must be nice,* she thought, *to pick up a phone and get whatever you want. Wish I could keep him on my side for a few months. He already has me jumping to his tune, no different than all the others he manipulates.*

After he finished his calls, he turned to look at her, his six-foot-plus frame leaning on the bar. His voice was businesslike, and she could imagine what would happen if somebody tried to put something over on him. She shivered. *Mind your p's and q's, Stacy.*

"I'll be gone two or three hours, Stacy. We'll go to dinner later, if that's okay with you." He smiled at her. "Somewhere you can wear jeans, all right?" He moved toward her. "Do whatever you feel like doing; stay here, if you'd rather."

He stood looking down at her, not touching her except with his eyes, which was enough to make her step backward. A smile touched his lips, and she stared, fascinated, at the tilt of the firm mouth above the almost dimple in his chin. "Don't run from me, Stacy." His hands rested on her hips, long fingers meeting behind her. Without thought, her hand went upward to his face, her forefinger touching the indentation that had caught her attention the first time she saw him. Concentrating on his features, she gazed

Miracles Take Longer

past her finger, past the straight nose, to the navy blue eyes, shadowed by thick black lashes as he looked down at her. She stood on tiptoe to meet his kiss, both hands on his shoulders.

His breath on her lips was warm just before his mouth settled on hers. He followed the curve of her lips, kissing with soft touches across to the corner of her mouth. As he drew away from her, her eyes flew open, questioning, but it was just a moment till his mouth came hard and demanding against hers. She drew in her breath, leaving her mouth warm and open beneath his, and he searched with slow deliberation for the response he wanted. For an instant she wished for more experience in lovemaking, but there was no need.

He held her just far enough away from him that his lips barely touched hers, and eyes wide open, she stared into the navy blue depths of his. A sparkle there made her wonder if the light from her own bewildered gaze was reflected back at her.

"Move close to me, Stacy," he whispered, his warm breath in her mouth as he spoke.

"I—I can't," she said. "I'm already—" she stopped speaking as his hands curved around her slim hips, lifting her up and forcing her body into the outline of his.

"Yes, you can. There's lots of room. Relax and see how easy it is."

She stopped trying to keep from touching him and leaned toward his body, feeling the hardness of his thighs supporting her.

"That's better," he said, and his mouth came hard

on hers, and there was no protest left in her. It was easy to believe that this was her first kiss, and she wished there was no end to it.

When Greg lifted his head, releasing only her mouth, her eyes drifted up to the darkness of his and saw a question there that was erased as he released her and let his hands slide down her arms to her wrists.

"I think October will be a long time coming." His lazy smile did a multitude of odd things to her heartbeat.

Stacy elected to stay in the apartment until Greg's return. She stood in the middle of the living room after he left, her fingers resting on her mouth he had kissed as though it were a natural thing, and something they had done many times before. But Stacy hadn't kissed that way, not ever before, and it left her rocking with a scary feeling that could only be because it was new to her. Not new to Greg. He had done it many times, she knew, and yet, he made her feel as though it were different for him. *Just imagination, or wishful thinking, Stacy; he's had a world of experience.*

She moved slowly through the apartment, not touching anything. It was clean, not a particle of dust, and she guessed he had a dependable maid. It wouldn't matter at the Mati Reservation. You could dust the makeshift tables and chairs made from canvas wraps every two minutes and the dust would still be fingertip deep, the grit from blowing sand sifting through the thin walls of tar and newspaper.

In the kitchen she paused at the refrigerator and opened it. The deep shelf held two cartons of milk and a bottle of Chianti. Six small bottles of Coca-Cola

Miracles Take Longer

stood upright and next to them, a carton of cream cheese. She didn't look in the crispers or meat tray, but took one of the Cokes and opened it with a bottle opener she found in the top drawer of the cabinet beneath the counter.

She avoided the two bedrooms she figured were farther down the hall, staying in the kitchen to finish the drink. She placed the bottle in the kitchen sink and returned to the living room. The long day was catching up with her and she was tired and sleepy. Taking off her boots, she stretched out on the carpeted floor, uneasy about going into a stranger's bedroom—although he wouldn't be a stranger for long if things went the way they were going. *I don't know how I ever got into this,* she thought, feeling skeptical about the whole weird deal. It was two hours later when she woke, trying to decide what she was doing in the strange apartment. She was still lying there, staring at the ceiling, when she heard the key turn in the door, and before she could get up Greg was standing looking down at her.

"I have beds," he told her, an odd smile curving his mouth.

She stood before he could reach down for her. There was no need to tell him the floor was great compared to what she slept on at the reservation, and there were no bugs competing for the space she occupied.

It was getting dark as they left the apartment to go to dinner.

The restaurant he took her to was near the edge of the city; people were dressed in all types of clothing from the elegant to her casual jeans. Greg talked easily about the weather, his job, her nurse's training, giving the indication he was unaware she wore faded jeans, not Dior originals.

"Are you going to stay with VISTA in another state, Stacy?" he asked as they had a last cup of coffee after dinner.

She shook her head. "I'm going back to regular nursing," she told him. "I'm not equipped to fight all the social problems I see." She stared into her cup, thinking of all she'd like to do, but knowing her limitations.

"No one person can undo all the injustices, Stacy. You'll have to accept that fact." He was studying her face, his eyes narrowed.

She nodded. "Yes, but—" She let the sentence drop and smiled at him. "The dinner was very good. Thank you."

His eyes widened, as though her comment were unexpected. He seemed about to say something, but changed his mind, accepting the check from their waiter, and holding the chair until she slid out to stand beside him. He was many inches above her in height, and she moved away to minimize the contrast in their sizes, having no idea why she felt she must. He dominated everything and everyone, not only her, she decided.

The drive back to Greg's apartment was almost totally silent, and she was hesitant to try to figure out what was coming next. He had said he would stay somewhere else, but he could very well change his mind and decide to stay in the apartment. Perhaps he

Miracles Take Longer 45

would demand payment from her before he delivered the money. Her thoughts were interrupted as he parked the car and came around to open her door. Holding hands, they walked to the building. It was after ten and no one was in the hallways as they waited for the elevator. The door slid open in front of them and they entered the empty car. He stood with his arm around her and kept it there as they reached his floor and walked down the corridor to his apartment. Unlocking his door, he stepped aside to let her enter the room, where he had left a light on.

She stood just inside the door, waiting, but he didn't go past her and she turned, eyes questioning him as they stood by the door.

He was leaning carelessly against the wall, watching her, his eyes shadowed so that she couldn't tell any of what he might be thinking.

"Want me to stay?" he inquired, his voice quiet, giving no indication if he wanted to stay or if he thought she expected him to do so.

The tip of her tongue sought the corner of her mouth in a nervous movement that didn't go unnoticed by the man she faced. He straightened away from the wall and was in front of her before she could think. He took her clenched fists from behind her, brought them up between them, loosening her fingers with his thumbs, then raising her hands so they fit on his shoulders. Her face was inches below his, but as he pulled on her arms she came up on tiptoe, putting her head back to allow her mouth to reach his. As their lips met, her body jerked, protesting, but he wasn't through with her yet.

He whispered, "Stacy," and his arms drew her tense figure into the shape of his body, needing her and wanting her to share that need. The rough stubble of his beard scraped a little as he moved his mouth back and forth on hers till her lips parted, and he was quickly inside the warm moistness, the tip of his tongue going under her upper lip over the smooth edge of her teeth.

She moaned, trying to close her mouth, but liquid mercury scorched through her veins and Greg's hands wouldn't let her go. One hand held her chin, forcing her mouth to remain on his, the other hand spread over her hip, fingers digging into its curving fullness.

His hold on her grew gentle and he held her close, releasing her mouth, pulling her face against his shirt-front. "I'd better say good night, Stacy," he whispered.

She didn't move, but nodded her head. He pushed her back to look down into her half closed eyes, smiling. "Sleep well, and I'll see you early tomorrow."

She was tempted to ask him to stay in the apartment with her. After all, there were two bedrooms. But she couldn't make her lips form the words, and quickly Greg turned to leave, smiling as he checked the lock and shut the door. She stood, her head to one side, listening, but there was no sound on the thick carpet as he walked away.

She wandered down the hall to the bathroom off the smaller bedroom, undressing to wrap a big towel around her. She rinsed out her underthings and looked around the room. It was as big as any room she had ever lived in, and drawers lined one side, holding linens. She found an extra hanger in the closet, hanging her freshly laundered pants and bra so they would be dry by morning. In one of the drawers she found pajamas, hopefully Greg's, and chose a pair of pale green ones, dropping the bottoms back into the drawer. She could use the top as a nightshirt; it was plenty long enough to cover her bottom.

She stood outside the shower, reading all the knobs giving instructions for their use. All she wanted was warm water. Why in the world were there so many nozzles? She turned the knob she finally decided would give her warm water and stepped into the clean, tiled area. It had been a long time since she had used hot, running water. Her running water was the small stream the reservation was lucky enough to boast.

With the water adjusted to her liking, she stood under the spray for a long time, then sighed when she turned off the water and toweled herself dry. That was worth the whole trip, she thought, then amended. Maybe not—she still had to see how high her payments were going to be.

Greg's pajama top fell below her knees, the sleeves hanging almost as far. She rolled them up, buttoned the top button, and climbed into the bed with fresh smelling sheets. Such luxury, she thought. Quickly she fell asleep, and did not even dream.

She eyed the shower the next morning, giving in with a grin, to get under the sparkling clean water. There was no telling how long before she got this chance again. She had dressed when Greg called.

"I'll pick you up in half an hour, Stacy, and we'll have breakfast. By that time the bank will be open." He hesitated and when she only murmured her thanks, he asked, "Did you sleep well?"

"Yes. And your water bill will be higher this month."

"Why?"

"The showers that we have come once in the spring, and once in the fall if we're lucky," she told him, and heard his disbelieving laughter.

Chapter Three

Stacy was back on the reservation a month before she had time to think about her strange bargain. Dr. Grove returned, and contrary to being a mistake about the missing drugs and money, it was all too true. She confronted him with the questions his first day back on the reservation, and to her surprise, he didn't bother to deny anything.

He told his story in a voice totally without expression. His nephew, a graduate law student at Harvard University, was involved in underworld drugs, and to protect him, Dr. Grove used everything he could drain from all the posts to which he was assigned, and Stacy was amazed at the intricate assignments he had arranged for himself. Besides the Mati Reservation, there were three more larger settlements with a lot more money involved.

She listened in disbelief as Dr. Grove related an outline of the events that led him to take the small amount of money and drugs allotted to the Mati Reservation, and the larger amounts from the others.

"I never did understand how Brice could use drugs

in the first place," Dr. Grove told her, his head in his hands. "He started in high school, all through college, and when he went on to Harvard, he was well hooked." He looked up, but Stacy had a feeling he didn't see her. "He's my only sister's boy, and when he came to me for help, I tried to get him off the drugs, but he wasn't interested, and it wasn't long before he got in with the sons of rich parents who could support a five-thousand-dollar-a-week drug habit. Brice couldn't, so he was introduced to the underworld drug traffic, getting deeper and deeper into debt. Now he's a lawyer trying to keep his sources for the drugs out of jail, and I'm trying to get out of debt and stay out of prison because of him."

Into the silence that followed, Stacy asked, "Why don't you ask Brice to repay some of the money you've spent on him?"

Dr. Grove's laugh was ugly. "He doesn't remember that he has an Uncle Brice, his namesake."

If she hadn't been so angry over his robbing the Indians, Stacy could have felt sorry for the doctor, but hardly believing what she had heard with her own ears, she left his office with a strong desire to throw up.

She went in search of Star, needing a witness to the bald admission the doctor was supplying. The torn plastic curtain separating her work area from the classroom was partly pushed aside, and she walked through, stopping short in surprise.

Star was leaning against the two sawhorses and rough planks that served as her desk, his arms pulling Rachel to him, and she watched in openmouthed fascination as he bent to kiss her, murmuring words she knew were his native Indian dialect. Rachel stood still until his hands urged her closer, then her arms went around Star's neck, and the lovers' embrace was complete.

Stacy backed out the door, retracing her steps to the path that led away from the school compound. She smiled to herself; the thought that Star and Rachel were in love filled her body with pleasure. That was right, she thought. That was exactly right.

Since the one kiss Star had given her in anger many months ago, he had never in any way tried to interest her in more than a friendly relationship after he had accepted the fact that she was trying to help, not hurt, his people. They had grown to be very close friends and that was enough. That he and Rachel had found each other was icing for the cake.

Greg was the driving force behind the fast action that took place in the next few weeks, calling Washington and talking to the powers that be who had reacted with lightning efficiency, already having Dr. Grove scheduled for a hearing. More and more Stacy wondered what kind of man she was involved with. One more month to complete her year's service with VISTA, and she would find out.

The two months between her meeting Greg Fields and the end of September were busy ones for Stacy. She was still trying to keep the few good things going for the Mati, teaching the few children the economics of life when she had little of concrete value to show them. Frustration at how little improvement she had made in their way of life went deep and she found herself growing angry even with Greg because he was so obviously among the chosen of the haves and have nots.

He had visited her a few times and as he walked or rode with her in the desolate surroundings, his dark blue eyes had missed little, but she knew that he blamed the Indians, for the most part, for the conditions in which they lived.

"They can always hold council, Stacy, and elect a representative to present their problems to Washington."

"I'm their representative, Greg," she told him, anger bringing sparks to her eyes. "Where have all my presentations ended?" She turned on him. "Let me tell you where they are. Buried under the Bureau of Indian Affairs red tape or lost in the bureaucratic shuffle in Washington."

Greg watched her, taking in the small body that could stiffen in outrage when someone made an uncomplimentary remark about the Indians. "Has anyone ever asked where you got eyes of such an impossible shade, Stacy?"

She flared. "No one cares, Greg."

"I'm very curious. They're most unusual." His smile was lazy, ignoring her outburst.

She stared at him, wondering why she even bothered. The money he gave her was gone, buying the medical supplies she thought the most important, plus a few staple groceries. And she still had to pay for it. She swallowed, watching him as he came toward her, and as he reached for her, she went up on tiptoes, her lips parted, wanting his kiss that she had known for such a short time. His arms, linked loosely around her waist, tightened to pull her up to him, his body lean and hard against hers. His lips touched her nose, moving to the corner of her mouth where the tip of his tongue probed just inside. She turned her head to get the fullness of his kiss, but he held her away, teasing her. She looked into his navy blue eyes, seeing them darken even more as he kissed her hard, holding the kiss until she whimpered and he released her.

"Sweet Stacy," he murmured against the heavy braids and, turning her, walked with his arm loosely around her waist, saying good-bye as soon as they were back within the compound. Her emotions where Greg was concerned were new and unfamiliar, causing moments of uneasiness when she took time to try to analyze what they might mean. It was these feelings that filled her as she watched his truck disappear in a cloud of dust.

As her year with VISTA drew to a close, Stacy was glad it was over. She felt like she had eaten half the compound at least twice a day, and was tired of not enough of anything except misery. Maybe, after this, she thought, the Bureau will take a little more notice of things, but she held little hope for that dream. She looked around at the dreary landscape. She would miss Star and Rachel, Dade, Allie, and the rest of the family, but most of it she could do without easily.

What would Greg do with her? Keep her in his apartment? Or would he rather she stayed somewhere else and visit his apartment on call? On call? A virgin call girl at age twenty-five. She giggled. How on earth had she gotten into this mess? *Poor Greg,* she sympathized to herself. *You will doubtless not get your money's worth.*

A mixture of feelings surged through her as she let her thoughts play with the memory of Greg's kisses. He was experienced in the ways of bringing out all the best responses in a woman, knew how to handle them with the tenderness every woman needed. Even so, he made love to her in a way that made her believe he was thinking only of her as his hands caressed her slim body, his lips teasing and tasting hers, promising fulfillment such as she had never known.

In contrast, her experience was skimpy, to say the least. Heavy petting had never been a problem for her, but she realized now that it was the men she had dated, few that there were. Greg could make her want things she hadn't thought of before, so that she no longer doubted her ability to belong to him for three months, but questioned his satisfaction for repayment of his loan.

With her mind on a million things, Stacy had little time to worry about the strange bargain that would soon have to be settled, but the time came when necessity forced her to do just that. She wondered at Greg's side of the deal, knowing he could have his choice of female company from a wide and varied selection. Would he change his mind? If so, what then? She pushed her fingers through her thick hair she had shampooed and was sitting in the sun to let it dry before braiding it. Smelling fresh as sunlight, it fell to her waist, and she remembered Greg's curiosity about the heavy braids, the touch of his hand as he caressed them, his hand contacting her breast enough for her to notice. She shivered there in the warm sun, realizing she had wanted more than just his touch. What desperation she must have felt to justify making the deal with Greg, so long ago it seemed at least one lifetime, with so many things happening. The trial and indictment. Appointment of Star as representative for the reservation. They had, at least, stirred up a few people for a little while.

She sighed, shook the heavy hair back from her face, pushing it over her shoulders. *I've never slept with a man. What will it be like? After three months, when he's through with me, what then? I hope those pills work, but if they don't, it would be something to have a little boy who looks like Greg. No, a little boy needs a father. You can't do that to him.* The troubling thoughts cut her off from her surroundings, and she looked around in surprise when a car door slammed nearby. She watched Greg walk toward her straight out of her thoughts, the trim tailored jeans and close-fitting blue knit shirt accented by his long-legged stride. A light-coloured straw Stetson was pushed carelessly back on the dark hair.

She was conscious of her cut off shorts, T-shirt that had once been yellow, and bare feet. He was grinning as he reached her.

"Caught you with your hair down," he said, stopping a few feet from her. "You did tell me you're twenty-five, didn't you?"

"Hello, Greg. Yes, I'll soon be twenty-six."

He shook his head. "I want to see your birth certificate; you look fourteen." His hand went out to touch her hair, dry now and lifted lightly by the warm desert breeze.

"Is there somewhere we can talk?" he asked.

"Let's ride down by the river. It's cooler there." She got her moccasins and borrowed a horse for him.

They rode past the school compound, westward to the high mesa where most of the reservation could be seen, and down to the canyon that sloped off to the small stream of water.

Greg sat the horse as though he had been born a cowboy. He turned in the saddle, smiling, waiting for her to come alongside of him, and she realized her first appraisal of him had been wrong. He got that beautiful tan from out of doors where he spent most of his time, not in a luxurious clubhouse, as she had suspected.

As an architect, he didn't spend much time behind that big slate-topped desk, but visited all the sites where he had work going. Stubbs, whom he had introduced on a visit to the Mati with Greg, turned out to be his right-hand man, second only to Greg in their company. Between the two of them, they covered all the continental United States and territories in their business of building and design.

As she reined her pony at his side, she admitted to the male magnetism he held for her, and she returned his smile, feeling a tremor inside at the look she encountered. He didn't speak, but guided the animal alongside hers, their legs almost touching. She let her thoughts wander to the intense awareness of her feelings for Greg, growing in a direction she couldn't control. *I could be heading for some real trouble,* she thought. She pressed her lips together and turned away from that line of thinking. *If he can help me get Star and Rachel on the right road, I'll owe him—whatever he demands.* The deal was made and beyond changing.

Greg pulled the reins of his horse, swung long legs over the saddle, dropping to the ground near her. He reached, and she slid into his arms, her body coming to rest against him, and he held her there, his face even with hers, his eyes looking directly into hers, his breath warm on her cheek as he closed the distance between them, touching gently, forcing her lips apart. He let her body slide down his, bending his head to hold the kiss as her feet touched the powdery red desert sand. Tiny spangles of fire spread from her stomach through her thighs as he pressed her hips closer to him.

"Stacy?" His voice was a whisper but there was strength and demand in the questioning of her name.

She didn't answer and he let her go, turning to lead her to an outcropping rock, then holding her hand as she sat down. He looped the horses' reins over another rock and sat beside her.

"Are you satisfied with the indictment, Stacy?"

She shook her head. "What I'd really like to do is stamp my feet and scream, and then sit down and have a good cry." She drew up her shoulders and let her breath out. "They didn't solve anything. And, if it weren't for you, the people here still wouldn't have the supplies they should have." She turned to look at him. "I appreciate your generosity and want to thank you for everything."

He smiled at her. "I want more than your appreciation and thanks, Stacy."

She didn't look away, but nodded. "Yes, of course."

"When will you be finished here?"

"The first of October."

He was quiet for a moment, but his eyes held hers. "Do you want me to pick you up next Friday?"

"No. I have some things I have to do. Tell me where to meet you and what time."

He studied her face, realizing she was pale under the smooth tan. "Come to the apartment. Can you be there by eight?"

"Yes. I'll be there."

The silence closed in around them as he continued to watch her. Not touching her with his hands, he leaned to kiss her, setting off a slow, easy thrill through her body. He lifted his head to look into her eyes, and pulled her close to him. This time his lips were hard and demanding, and she answered his demands with all her pent-up feelings behind it. Greg pushed her away, his breath uneven against her cheek.

"Not here, Stacy." She kept her face against his throat, not wanting to look at him. He kissed the tip of her nose. "Till Friday." His hand smoothed the long hair brushing his cheek.

All her paperwork was finished by late Wednesday. Star and Rachel drove her into Phoenix on Thursday morning in the battered old truck Star kept wired together and running most of the time, dropping her at the YWCA, only a few blocks from Greg's apartment. She watched the truck disappear around the corner of the block with misgivings, wondering if she had accomplished any one thing while she was on the reservation. At least, Rachel and Star found they belonged together, and that had to be a plus. She smiled and turned to her small pile of belongings, getting them into the tiny room that would be her home for a while, until she could find a job.

She rented a Post Office box and mailed applications and résumés to several addresses. She had to get back to a paying job, and get on with her schooling, she thought. Most of her savings from Philadelphia General had been spent on the reservation, and there was about enough left to last till pay day, if pay day wasn't too far away.

FRIDAY, five minutes to eight. Stacy bit her lip and stood looking at the door to Greg's apartment. She wore a light Windbreaker over her jeans and shirt because the weather had turned a little cooler. *I should have something slinky for this rendezvous, but he'll have to accept what I have. In everything.*

The door opened as soon as her light knock hit. Greg's smile was warm as he reached for her hand. "Hello, Stacy. Come on in."

Somehow, the apartment looked different in the evening near-darkness. The instant-on lamps were softly shaded, and music came from hidden speakers. Unbidden resentment choked her for a moment. Some people lived like kings, never knowing want, while others struggled to survive. What was supposed to be fair about that?

It had nothing to do with her. She made the debt in

good faith, now the time for paying was at hand, whether she was ready or not. The goods were delivered, and payment was due.

Greg walked past her to the bar, turned to watch her as she sat, stiffly upright, in the club chair farthest from him. "Relax, Stacy," he said, smiling. "How about a drink for the special occasion?"

Sarcasm? She couldn't be sure. "All right," she finally managed to say.

He handed her a small delicate glass with amber-colored liquid in it. "Brandy. Sip it slowly," he cautioned her.

She put it to her lips, inhaling the sharply pleasant aroma. She touched her tongue to the brandy, gasping at the sting, but it warmed her mouth. She needed a gallon to warm her all over, she thought, trying to keep from shivering.

Greg sat on the couch facing her, long fingers of both hands clasped around the glass he held. The white knit shirt, open to show his brown throat, stretched across his shoulders as he leaned toward her. Black linen slacks were taut over his hard muscled thighs. With a flick the black lashes came up, dark blue eyes surprising her green ones going over him.

"Where are you going, now that your year with VISTA is up?"

She shook her head. "I have in some applications, no offers. I want to go somewhere I'll never be cold again." She thought of the cold wind blowing the desert sand through the compound, the nights she slept fully dressed to keep warm. "There are lots of good opportunities back east, but I don't really want to go back there."

"Don't you have family back there?"

"No, there's only me." She smiled to let him know it didn't matter. There was a time when she had wished for a family, but it no longer bothered her that she was alone.

He regarded her without speaking, studying the small, tanned face beneath the dark coils of hair, a startling contrast to the deep eyes. She had made no pretense at dressing to show off her rather thin figure, having nothing that would do justice to a man of Greg's taste in women's finery. The shirt she wore was pale blue cotton. Instead of boots, she wore new leather moccasins Rachel had made for her as a going-away present.

He placed his glass on the table in front of him, leaned back on the couch, and said, "Come over here, Stacy."

She stiffened, and her mouth went dry. Softly spoken, it was still a command and she stared at him, knowing what was coming.

He waited, and when she neither moved nor spoke, he said, "Stacy?"

She didn't have a lot of choice and stood up to walk on stiff legs around the edge of the table to stand in front of him. He caught her hand, tugging, till she sat beside him, pulling her back into his arms.

She tipped her head back, looked into the dark blue eyes so close to her own. It was a mistake. She watched his mouth curve in the beginning of a smile. He kept his hand against her cheek, holding her face close to his. Their lips met, his gently questioning as they forced hers apart. The sharp thrill hit the bottom of her stomach with unexpected force, and she stiffened.

"No," he whispered. "Not like that. Like this."

He took the brandy glass from her hand and placed it on the table beside his, all without releasing his hold on her. The freed hand went around her waist, bringing her body against him. His mouth searched hers, and suddenly she was responding. Her arms went around his neck, the parted lips answering his demands.

She closed her eyes to the sweetness filling her body, a new experience, and desire for which she had no name. Quicksilver slid along each nerve, jangling awake the long sleeping desire no man had yet discovered. She had only had a preview when Greg first kissed her, and this was different—so different as to be unrecognizable as the same emotion. Her breath quickened as he lay back on the couch, pulling her on top of him, holding her so she knew the change in his body.

Lowering her face to his, she let the tip of her tongue trace his mouth, and as the burning sensation shook them both, she moaned and whispered, "Greg?"

He held her there, not letting her kiss him, his eyes wide open, looking into her face. "Say it again," he told her, his fingers tightening on her shoulders.

"What?" Not understanding, she felt surprise part her lips.

"My name. You've never said my name before."

She didn't speak for a moment, her gaze going

from his dark hair, over the rugged features, to his mouth, to the near dimple in his chin.

"Greg?" Her lips went to the dimple, the tip of her tongue caressing it. He turned his head and their kiss went deep, their bodies blending together. When she thought she would never move again, he pushed her away, sitting up to hold her, to look at the pale, golden face, her lips like pink crushed satin, parted enough to show the edge of white teeth.

"Sweet Stacy," he whispered. "Baby." He gathered her in his arms, and long strides took them down the hall to an open door. Inside he stood her on her feet, his arms supporting her. His hand beneath her chin forced her face upward so that she was looking straight into his eyes. His mouth came bruisingly against hers, his body tightly fitted to her own.

He turned her, and the bed gave as he sat on the edge, pulling her with him, rolling over so that she landed in the middle of the king-size bed. Greg's breath was ragged as his mouth found the cleft between her small breasts, his fingers busy undoing the buttons of her shirt. She felt her bra give beneath his fingers, and he pushed the skimpy garment away to gain access to the creamy mounds of flesh.

She gasped as his warm lips closed over the hard brown tip of her breast, and her body arched against his. Desire was an ache in the pit of her stomach, and she swung her leg across him, pressing closer into his hard thighs.

When he released the hard nipple, his hands were already moving down her body, the belt came loose, and the jeans zipper posed no problem for him since she did not resist. It seemed only an instant until she lay beside him in loose bra and panties. It was then that he pulled away enough to see her eyes, as his hands slid just beneath the elastic.

Under his breath, she heard him swear. Almost in a whisper he said, "You're a virgin!" It was a statement—not a question.

Not moving, she answered him, wondering at the expression in his eyes. "Yes."

"Why didn't you tell me?"

She stifled a giggle. "Why? You didn't ask my qualifications when the bargain was made."

"I took it for granted you knew your way around. Any girl who is a registered nurse, twenty-five years old, asking me to do what you did with anything I asked in return, no holds barred—" He moved his shoulders. "There was no way I could know that you'd never been around at all."

"What made you stop now? How could you tell by just holding me without—without—?" She hesitated.

He looked at her for a long moment, then rolled away from her, stood up, and walked away from the bed. "The way you came into my arms, you came so willingly—I would have sworn you knew what you were doing. I thought you wanted me too, but when you knew what was happening, you froze solid." He ran long fingers through his short hair, shaking his head. "No woman who wants a man and knows what she's doing would do that. You're either awfully naive or you make your plans well—which is it, Stacy?" His voice hardened. "I'll have to give you credit anyway, for a while I thought I was on the winning side." He

Miracles Take Longer

stared down at her, cold dislike in his face. "You can leave now."

She shook her head. "I've always paid my debts and that's what I plan to do now."

"Shut up and get out of here," he told her through clenched teeth, his eyes going over her.

She didn't move. "You're right, you know. I do want you. It's the only time in my life I've felt that way about a man. Teach me what I should know. I have to learn from someone, sometime, and it might as well be you."

His blue gaze raked her from the desperate eyes, the slender near-naked body, to the strong tanned legs. "I want a woman, not a child." His voice grated. He moved swiftly, catching her arm, pulling her from the bed, dragging her across the room till they stood in front of the full-length mirror. He turned her to face the mirror, her body against his. Her bra had dropped away, and she stared at their reflection, seeing his dark good looks, the angry eyes, the mouth a straight, hard line.

"Look at you, Stacy. What man in his right mind would knowingly be the first?" He put her arm to her side so she had to see her body.

She refused to look at her reflection, watching him instead. "What happened to the man who looked for a virgin to marry?" she asked.

"I don't want to marry you; I just want you," he came back at her.

She drew a ragged breath, pushed his arms away, and walked out of range of the mirror. She crossed her arms over her small rounded breasts. "Greg, listen, you're looking at this all wrong. It was a business arrangement. You fulfilled your part of the bargain; now it's my turn." She looked straight at him. His uncompromising gaze locked with hers.

Her chin went up, and her voice wasn't more than a whisper. "Maybe I don't have a number-ten body, but it would be yours alone, for whatever that's worth."

"You're the one who doesn't understand, Stacy," he told her, his voice quiet now. "Put your clothes on and I'll take you home." He turned at the door. "I'll mark your bill paid in full so your conscience will rest easy." He was gone, closing the door behind him.

She dressed with shaky hands, her brain and body numb and barely functioning. She looked around the room, seeing for the first time the king-size bed where the print of their bodies showed on the snowy spread, a bookcase headboard filled with books on architecture, solar energy, and conservation.

Who would want to be the first with you? he had asked. Or last?

Her moccasined feet made no noise as, stumbling a little, she went down the hall, through the kitchen door, and down the stairs, not even thinking of the elevator. Reaching the ground floor, she left through the rear entrance. Her jacket was still in Greg's closet, and she shivered as the chill wind hit her. She ran the few blocks to the YWCA, got through the deserted lobby, and to her small alcove on the second floor. She shivered, unable to stop shaking, as she undressed and crawled beneath the light covers. It was daylight when she finally drifted into a troubled sleep.

Morning gave her no answers to the million questions she needed answered, first and foremost: What now? Although she failed to repay Greg, he probably considered her good riddance. He had more experienced toys he could play with, leaving the babies for someone else.

It was Wednesday before she remembered the Post Office box she had rented, and found a few letters, mostly advertisements. Her heart jumped. Phoenix Medical Center asked for an interview.

HER INTERVIEW with Phyllis Dorn, Superintendent of Nurses at the Center was over in half an hour. "Do you have any local references, Stacy?"

Stacy shook her head, not about to mention one Greg Fields. "The only people who know me are the ones on the reservation. The doctor who was there isn't available." She held her breath, wondering if Mrs. Dorn had read anything in the papers.

Evidently not, or she didn't make any connection with Stacy, for she told her, "That's all right. I can call Philadelphia General. They should still have your records on file." She stood up to indicate the interview was finished. "Go get your physical and report to me Monday at three." The shortage of nurses was in her favor.

Stacy didn't mind the three-till-eleven evening shift as so many nurses did. She moved into the nurses' dormitory on the hospital grounds and went on with her conservative way of life. Mornings she read or walked, went to the library, and back to her room in time to dress for work. It was hard work, and she slept well when she finished her shift, refusing to think about Greg and her aborted attempt to repay his loan. Her duty shifts changed and she adjusted easily to the different hours, but was delighted when Dr. Haw, a surgeon she had assisted several times, requested she be assigned to work with him in the operating room for three months, which meant all day shifts.

She left the OR on Friday at three, a two-day weekend ahead of her to do as she pleased, a rare bonus. *I could rent a car and go see Rachel and Star,* she thought, crossing the yard to the dormitory. She stood a moment, watching the traffic through the misty rain of a warm, early December day. Christmas would soon be here, and she still needed a few things for the reservation.

She sighed and went into the hallway, checking her mail slot. Taking the stairs two at a time, she rounded the landing and collided with two figures descending the steps. Hands steadied her as she looked up. Shock kept her rooted to the spot, staring into navy blue eyes. Greg continued to hold her, neither of them speaking.

"Well, Waring, if you're ready, we'll move." It was Dr. King, Director of the Center.

"Oh, excuse me." Breathless, Stacy extracted herself from Greg's hands and stepped aside.

The two men went on, talking as before, but she was still standing there, holding her breath, when Greg looked back at her. Somehow she got to her room, but it was a long time before her body stopped trembling.

I don't know why I got so excited, she thought. *He looked totally unimpressed.* She sat looking out the window at the rain, decided it was not the weekend to go to the reservation. She got her bedraggled all-weather coat and walked to the library a mile away. She found the books she needed to help in her upcoming tests and tried to study.

Later, thoughts of Greg intruded until she gave up and went to bed to lie awake, twisting and turning. He had no way of knowing that he had brought to life the awareness of a woman for a man, awakened a desire her inexperience had never prepared her for. She pushed away the memory of his lovemaking, but her body refused to forget.

Chapter Four

Phoenix seldom got rain the way it was pouring when she awakened. A walk in the rain was a luxury, so she got her coat and headed downstairs. The telephone in the hall rang as she passed, and she detoured a few steps to answer it. No one believed that nurses needed to sleep late on weekends.

"Waring," she said into the mouthpiece. There was brief silence, and a deep masculine voice said, "Good morning, Stacy."

She held the phone away to look at it, gulped, and said, "G-good morning, Greg."

He asked, as though they had said good-bye an hour ago, "Are you on your way out?"

"Just for a walk and coffee," she answered.

"I'm down the street at the drugstore. Can I pick you up?"

She hesitated, and he added, "Please?"

"All right." She took a deep breath, wondering at the panic she felt.

A few minutes later she ran to his car as he pulled

to the curb, tumbling in beside him. The car didn't move, so she looked across at him.

A slight smile touched his lips. "I thought you had disappeared forever. Why didn't you let me know where you're working?"

"It occurred to me that you would prefer not to know." She gave her attention to fastening the seat belt.

He pulled the car into the traffic. "Why would you think that?"

She studied his face without answering, except for a shake of her head.

"I checked the hospitals here the next week, but you hadn't filed an application at that time." When she still said nothing, he asked, "Have you had breakfast?"

"No."

He drove in silence for a few moments, and she made no attempt at conversation. "This okay?" he asked, as he turned into a parking lot by a small coffee shop.

"Yes." Her knowledge of restaurants was scant. The hospital dining room was cheap and nourishing, if not designed for the gourmet.

They dashed through the rain, and in dismay she remembered the well-worn coat covering jeans and white blouse. Clean was all you could say for them, but Greg seemed not to notice as he removed her coat and hung it behind her. Facing him in the cozy booth, she wet her lips, hiding her fists in her lap, then met his eyes and stiffened.

"Shall we go back to the beginning and start over?" His look traveled from the heavy braids, over her face, to her mouth, and back to meet her green eyes.

"What do you mean?"

"Do you have plans for tonight?"

She waited as the waitress placed coffee in front of them and took their order. "No. Unless you call studying chemistry formula plans."

One eyebrow lifted in the gesture she remembered so well. "Is that your entertainment, Stacy?"

"Mostly."

He shook his head. "You're still as informative as ever, I see. Can't you bring yourself to open up with me?"

She studied her coffee cup, thinking of their last encounter. "What do you want from me, Greg?" she asked.

"When you didn't follow me within a few minutes that night, I went looking for you, but you disappeared without a trace. I couldn't believe one little girl could vanish so completely." He leaned on the table. "Even Star and Rachel couldn't help, whether because they didn't want to or really didn't know is debatable."

"They didn't know for a while," she told him, surprised at his having gone that far to check, and remembering the period she shied away from any communication with anyone, busy trying to forget her experience with Greg. She no longer visited Mati every chance she got, not only because of studying, but she wanted Star and Rachel to make their own adjustments with the new VISTA representative. Since the overthrow of the Grove regime, they spoke for the reservation, things were working well, and Stacy was glad to let them have the reins, concentrating on getting rid of the bad taste the whole thing had left in her mouth. Their breakfast came and for a few moments they concentrated on the meal, Stacy aware of the difference in the meals here and in the plain hospital cafeteria. She waited while he paid the cashier, observing the attention he received from her.

As they left the restaurant the rain let up just enough till they reached the car, then seemed to come down with a vengeance. They sat enclosed in the soundproof shelter of the car, the rain drumming on the roof.

She tilted her head, listening to the steady pouring of the rain. Turning to Greg, she started to speak, only to find his face close to hers. His mouth touched hers, then lifted, as he gazed down at her. A tender smile touched his lips and his kiss was gentle, still demanding a response from her. Eyes closed, she didn't move for a brief moment but her body trembled as his warm mouth teased at her senses. Her fingers were hesitant on his throat, slowly moving to the back of his head as she pressed against his hard chest, pliant beneath his caressing hands.

He let her go, his hands touching her braids as he moved back behind the steering wheel and started the car. "The rain isn't supposed to last long," he said. "I have something to show you."

He drove northeast on the interstate for a few miles,

then turned north. Stacy wasn't familiar with this side of the city, so she watched with interest as the car began to climb the higher elevation. He turned the car from the paved road onto a gravel lane, and a thousand yards or so farther, stopped.

At first Stacy didn't see anything unusual, until he pointed to what looked like a boarded-up entrance in the side of the hill. The rain had stopped, and Greg led her around to the north side of the hill where they found another entrance. This one was fitted with strange-looking beige-colored panels slanting away from the small mountain.

"Watch your step, Stacy," he told her. "We still have panels lying around that haven't been installed."

She followed close behind him, gazing in amazement at what was inside the panels. The room they entered was at least five hundred square feet, and well lighted, but she saw no electric lights. He pointed to the high cathedral ceiling, where a huge skylight afforded the natural illumination, even though it was still partly cloudy. The floor was raw boards with thick insulation beneath them.

"I only have the master bedroom finished, and the kitchen, sort of," he said, walking through an arched doorway to his left. The rooms were underground, but in such a way that skylights could be built through the earthen roof.

She stared. She had heard about energy conservation, but she couldn't imagine a house built as this one was. They came to another heavy wooden door, and Greg pushed it inward, revealing a totally different world. Everything was built in. The king-size bed along one wall, covered with a heavy gold spread; a mirror hung over the drawers installed along the opposite wall. There were no windows, only the skylight in the domed ceiling. The floors were finished with dark gold plush carpet that her feet sank into.

"There's only basic electric wiring. It will require about five percent of regular usage." He walked to what looked like a solid wall, pushed a button, and the door slid back to reveal a bathroom, complete with dressing table and walk-in closet.

Stacy shook her head. "I can't even begin to understand how this works. I never understood the radio and telephone, so don't ask me to understand solar power."

Greg laughed. "It's easy enough if you just think about the basics. The best thing is it works."

"How long will it take you to finish it?" she asked.

"Four to six months. I have to wait on some special panels we build to specifications. That takes longer than anything else."

He led her back through the first room, down a narrow hallway, to the kitchen, a shiny stainless steel marvel. Cabinets were built around the walls; counters in the center with a microwave oven, double sink, and plenty of counter space. One wall opened to the south, covered with the paneling she now recognized as solar transmitters.

"What about hot weather?" she asked.

"It works in reverse to cool the same areas." Greg smiled at her obvious puzzlement.

"I'm glad some people are geniuses without depending on me." She looked around. "This is real privacy, and so quiet." She sighed. "Imagine studying in a place like this where you could concentrate without all the noise pollution."

"What are you studying for now, Stacy? I thought you had your degree."

"I want my Master's in Medical Science. I need it to go on to the special burn schools and some of the other special departments."

"Where are the schools?"

"San Antonio, Houston, or Atlanta." She let her hand slide across the sparkling counter. "It will take me a year."

He was leaning against the counter and captured her hand. "The schooling lasts a year?"

"No. It will take me that long earning the money as I go."

"How about a scholarship?" His gaze remained intent on her face.

"They don't have any that I know of." She smiled at him, trying to free her hand.

She watched his eyes darken as he pulled her close. Her head went back, and their lips met. For an instant his touch was gentle, then with bruising force he kissed her. Inside her Stacy felt the stirrings that had come to be familiar when she was with Greg. She stood straight against him, then with a sigh she relaxed. His hands moved down her arms, around her waist, over her hips, holding her immovable against him.

"Stacy?" Her name was a whispered question she didn't remember answering. She realized they were no longer in the kitchen, but she was stretched out on the big bed, Greg's body holding her there. She stared

Miracles Take Longer 77

into the face just above hers, wondering if the feelings she had through her body were those reflected in his eyes.

Her own eyes widened, and she said, "Greg?" She tried to move. "I don't— No."

"Yes, Stacy." His mouth came to hers, murmuring words she couldn't distinguish, and her body responded even as her mind objected. Her slender frame shook with the emotions he awakened, her arms around his neck, pulling his face to hers. Greg's eyes, shadowed by dark lashes, darkened as his fingers touched her face, the heavy braids, his lips following the same path until they found her mouth again. Tasting the sweetness of her lips, he moved on to her throat, the unbuttoned blouse revealing the cleft between her firm, rounded breasts. The tip of his tongue traced the curve of flesh over the lacy bra cup. Fire swept through her as she accepted the loving assault on her body. He lay beside her, pushing her jeans down over her hips, separating her legs, slim fingers stroking her thighs, feeling them quiver. His body arched upward as his hand behind her hips forced her to accept his hard thrust, moaning as he entered her.

A scalding pain tore through her thighs and she gasped, fighting to free herself, but his arms welded them together. He held her close, stroking her trembling body, murmuring reassurances until she grew still.

"I'm sorry, Stacy. That's why I didn't want to be first." His voice was gentle, vibrant with the emotion they both were feeling. "But I'm glad it was me."

She lay still, wondering at the pain that accompanied such sweetness. It was a long time later that she moved her face away from his throat, looked up into the dark blue eyes smiling at her. "Will it always be that way?"

"No, honey." He touched her mouth with gentle fingers. "I'll show you how sweet it can be." His hands soothed her taut body until she relaxed, whispering to her as his lips caressed her cheek, his hand moving over the flat belly to her thighs. She tried to pull away but he said, "No, Stacy, put your arms around me." And as she responded he said, "That's right. Now, love me, darling."

STACY'S FREE TIME became Greg's, and she visited the new house every chance she had, fascinated by her feelings for Greg and his attention to everything she wanted. She watched the building become a finished product, asking question after question about the cause and effect of solar energy. Greg took time to go over details that puzzled her, explaining his ideas as he put them to work.

Christmas was her best ever. She was on duty Christmas Eve and Greg picked her up at eleven and they went to his apartment where they had decorated the tree the week before. Gaily wrapped packages lay in multicolored disarray beneath the tree, some for Greta and Stubbs but most had tags with either Stacy or Greg on them.

She showered, putting on the jade-green gown and negligee Greg had given her a few nights before. When she returned to the living room, he had mixed drinks for them, making hers mild and sweet the way she liked them without much alcohol.

"Are Greta and Stubbs coming by?" she asked.

"No. They were going to Mass and we'll see them sometime tomorrow." He sat on the couch, pulling her down beside him. "I don't want to share you with anyone tonight."

Her head on his shoulder, she sighed, breathing in the scent that belonged only to Greg. He tilted her head back and kissed her full on the lips, his mouth lingering until her arms slid around his neck and her body stirred in slow motion against his. He lifted his head enough to whisper, "It's just past midnight. Merry Christmas, Stacy."

"Merry Christmas, Greg." Eyes half closed, she smiled. "Can we open presents now?"

He drew away from her in mock surprise. "How can you think of presents at a time like this?"

Her voice teasing, she said, "I guess I'm mercenary."

"In that case," he said, kissing her hard, then letting her go, "I guess we'd better open the presents and let you have your way because, afterward, I get to have mine." He smiled down at her as he stood up. "Deal?"

"Deal," she agreed, following him to the tree, sitting on the floor as he picked up a small package.

"Must be yours," he said. "It isn't big enough for me."

She took it, untying the gold string and pulling the tiny card from it to read: To Stacy, From Greg. Her fingernail slid beneath the tape and the paper came away from a small box. She pushed the top from it to reveal a thin gold serpentine chain. "Oh, Greg, it's beautiful," she said as he leaned over to fasten it around her neck where it glittered against her throat. Her lips were moist and parted as he gave her a brief hard kiss. "I'll wear it always."

It was her turn to hand Greg a package, somewhat bigger than hers. Inside the blue and silver paper was another box. He pulled the sides apart and took out a tobacco humidor and pipe rack with two slim pipes in the holders.

He whistled. "Where'd you get that?"

"Dr. King flew to New York last week and got it where he buys all his pipes and tobacco."

Greg placed the gift on the floor and turned to reach for her, pulling her down with him as he stretched out on the carpet. His hands moved up and down her arms, each move bringing her body closer until she was lying almost on top of him. "Sweet," he murmured.

Her body tensed as he caressed her hips, pressing her into his hardening muscles. Still new at the art of lovemaking, she was unsure how to respond to Greg's demands and breathless at the feelings he awakened in her.

"Don't fight me, Stacy," he said, his lips on the warm shadowy cleft beneath the lace of her gown. He pushed a strap aside, exposing the pale firmness of her breast and his mouth covered the rosy tip, his tongue roughly teasing until it grew hard. As he moved to her other breast her body trembled and her breathing became harsh.

"You want me, Stacy?" he asked.

"Yes, yes, Greg. Take me now darling." Her fingers dug into him as her body arched and he fitted himself between her thighs.

GREG MADE TRIPS out of town, leaving his car for Stacy to drive out to "The Place" where she could study in the quiet and peace of the desert. She couldn't wait to see the house when it was finished but never minded staying there in the various stages of completion.

Finding her somewhere in the big house studying, Greg would pick her up, carry her slim body with ease to the king-size bed, and make love to her until they were both breathless. If he was working over a weekend, they stayed in his apartment, but Stacy preferred the wild, lonely desert. Greg's arms was the place she enjoyed most, wherever he was, and his promise had come true. He taught her how unbearably sweet his loving could be. She forgot she was repaying a loan.

February brought springlike temperatures to Phoenix, and Stacy felt the change within her body. Saturday morning, she lay staring at the domed ceiling of Greg's bedroom, when beside her, she felt him stir. She turned to look at him; his dark blue eyes stared back at her.

She raised herself on an elbow and touched his face. "I'm going to have a baby."

His eyes dilated, the only change of expression on Greg's face. "You're sure?"

She nodded. "Seven weeks."

"Ah, Stacy, you'd think a registered nurse would be informed about birth control."

"I know. When I expected to sleep with you, I was

taking the pill. When you threw me out, I stopped." She drew a quivering breath. "I started back to taking them, but it was too late."

"What do you plan to do?" His arm moved to lie across her stomach. "An abortion?"

"No."

"Then what?"

"I'll have her."

"Her?" His quiet voice was almost idle in his inquiry.

She looked at him, a smile beginning at the corner of her mouth. "Yes, her. And I'll tell her all the things she needs to know before she's turned loose in the world. I wouldn't want her to be as dumb as I was." She lay back against the pillow, remembering a childhood that wasn't what she wanted for her baby; no love, no one to pet you when you don't understand, when you stub your toe, when you need a kiss to ease the pain; no one to care that your first day at school was frightening to a nearly six-year-old. No one to fix a peanut butter sandwich when you're hungry. No one.

"My baby will have a mother," she told him with quiet intensity.

"If it's a boy?" he asked her.

She shook her head. "No, I'll have a girl."

He pulled her into his arms, pushing the heavy braids back over her shoulder. "Are you afraid?"

"Not yet." She lay against him, feeling the strong beat of his heart beneath her hand.

He kissed her temple, his lips moving to the lobe of her ear. "We'd better make arrangements to get married next week."

Miracles Take Longer

For a moment she was still, then she moved to look at him. "Why?"

"It may be a boy and I'll need to tell him a few things. Either way, a baby needs a mother and a father, doesn't it?" He pulled a long braid toward him, bringing her body back to him. His mouth found hers, and the hardness of his kiss roused her as he knew it would.

Greg made all the arrangements for their wedding, engaging a judge, who was a golf-playing friend, to perform the civil ceremony. It would be performed in Greg's office with Greta and Stubbs as witnesses.

They were at dinner, Stacy quiet and subdued, wondering about the wedding scheduled the following day. She nor Greg had any family, but she felt no loss, since she had never had anyone, not even real close friends till she went to the reservation and met Star and Rachel. If circumstances had been different, she would have invited them but it didn't seem right, somehow, to celebrate a forced marriage.

She raised her eyes from the menu to see Greg watching her. He smiled. "Would you like to see your ring?"

Her eyes widened. She hadn't thought about a ring with her mind on so many other things. "Oh, could I?"

He waited until the hostess brought their coffee, then reached into his pocket, opened a small gray velvet box. Inside lay a circlet of diamonds in white gold, a narrow band of sparkling beauty.

"Give me your hand."

"But—" she started to protest.

He said with quiet assurance, "We need to see if it fits, Stacy. If not, I can have it adjusted tomorrow."

She stuck out her hand, spreading her fingers, and he slipped the ring on. It fit. After she saw the simple beauty of the ring on her hand, she was reluctant to let him have it back, but his smile convinced her, and she released it.

"It's beautiful, Greg."

THE SIMPLE MARRIAGE CEREMONY lasted only a few minutes and, legally, she belonged to Greg. Her mind strayed as the quiet words were spoken and she wondered again at the bargain she had made, and had royally messed up. She came back to the present as the judge said, "You may kiss the bride."

Greg's dark head bent to hers and he looked straight down into her eyes, causing her to blink, guessing that he couldn't tell how very much she loved him.

They turned to be congratulated by Greta and Stubbs. Greta was stunning in a pale yellow knit suit that clung to her faultless figure, showing off every feature to the best advantage. To her surprise Stacy decided Stubbs was handsome in a chunky sort of way. Though he was not much taller than Greta, his shoulders were wide, tapering to a slim waist; he wore a tailor-made suit of tan that complemented Greta's dress.

Hand on his arm, Stacy looked up at Greg. The navy blue suit he wore turned his eyes even darker and the light blue shirt against the smooth tanned skin emphasized his good looks.

The dress she was wearing had really been Greg's selection after he overcame her arguments on the price she thought was too much. He laughed at her as they finally agreed on a pale gray silk dress with a lavender scarf and belt, slippers and bag to match. What he didn't realize was that the price of that dress would pay for a month's allotment of medical supplies for the Mati Reservation.

With something like panic, Stacy realized she would soon be wearing maternity clothes. What kind of parents will we make? she wondered, looking up to meet Greg's glance. He saw her uncertainty, squeezed her hand he still held, and pulled her along with him.

"We're having dinner at the club, Stacy, then home and rest for you. You look tired."

It was almost midnight as Greta and Stubbs left them, calling congratulations, and Greg closed the door, turning to reach for her.

"Feel any different, Mrs. Fields?"

"Slightly overwhelmed, Mr. Fields."

He laughed, scooping her up to carry her into the bedroom they had shared so often.

Chapter Five

There was little to move from the nurses' dormitory to Greg's apartment. The faded blue cardboard suitcase she had had since high school held everything she owned, except her uniforms, which she kept separate from all other clothing. The white polyester picked up stains, and keeping them away from other materials and colors preserved the brightness.

"Can we live at the new place soon?" Stacy asked one evening as they sat, she studying, and Greg going over plans.

He looked up to smile at her. "Soon. There are people coming out from Washington to go over the workings. Then, Stubbs and I will finish up the front, and the other two bedrooms." He stood up and stretched. "You can move into 'The Place' in about a month."

He referred to the new house as hers because she loved it so much. The wide front lawn the landscapers had turned into a desert garden of huge white and red rock, saguaro and palm cactus, with fat barrel cactus squatted at intervals, and prickly pears with their huge red fruit decorating the earthy colors.

"How many courses do you need to finish your credits for your Master's, Stacy?" Greg asked, leaning over her shoulder to look at the book she held.

She thought a moment. "Two more, if I can get three hours each." She frowned. "I'll have to wait for them until after the baby comes."

"Can't you take them now, or is that too heavy a schedule?"

"Not really, but—" she hesitated.

"But what?" he questioned.

"I want to spend the money I have on special things for the baby." She smiled at him. "The degree will have to wait."

"I'll open an account for you tomorrow and you go ahead with your studies." He touched the braids lying on her shoulders. "Who knows? You may need all that knowledge to help look after the little tyke."

It seemed odd, taking Greg's money even though they were married. She had always paid her own way, frugal though it was, and was still willing to do so. She felt his having to marry her was all her fault, but he seemed not to mind, never reminding her in any way that he had other plans for his life.

The visitors from Washington came and they entertained them over a weekend. Oliver George was a contractor interested in energy conservation at airports around the country and was impressed by the house.

"You've kept your costs down considerably from anyone else we've talked to. How do you manage that with inflation hitting everyone, Greg?"

Greg launched into technical cost details and Stacy listened, as attentive as any of the men in the group. *I'm married to an extraordinary man,* she decided, remembering his handling of the Indian crisis for her. *He will, of course, make a very good father.*

She was on the eleven-till-seven in the morning shift when the house was completed enough for them to move in, and Greg, along with Stubbs and his crew, took care of all the moving. Greg kept the apartment in town, moving only his desk and office furniture into his study in the new place. By the time Stacy came home, everything was in place.

They walked arm in arm through the pleasant rooms, enjoying the quiet spacious areas, with ample light coming through the skylights in every room that wasn't completely underground.

He guided her away from their bedroom back toward the kitchen. "Are you very tired?" he asked.

"A little." She stretched. "I need to shower and get this hair washed."

"Later," he said and led her into the dining alcove off the kitchen.

She gasped, staring at the table set with pale gold linen napkins and cloth, a huge bowl of snapdragons and gladioli in the center, and a bottle of champagne resting in a silver ice bucket.

"Have you ever had champagne and caviar for breakfast?" he asked, bending to kiss the back of her neck.

She turned to him, lifting her arms, her green eyes bright with laughter. She wrinkled her nose and shook her head. "Sounds awful."

He laughed. "Spoilsport. Scrambled eggs and champagne?"

She nodded. "Some better."

He pulled out her chair and, as she sat down, slipped it back to the table, leaning across her to get the small crystal glass by her hand. She jumped as the cork popped from the bottle, and he smiled, handing her the glass half filled with bubbling pink liquid. He poured a like amount in his glass and sat down at the end of the table.

"To us, Stacy, and a solid earthen roof over our heads."

She smiled. "To us, Greg, and a solid earthen floor beneath us." He touched his glass to hers and leaned to kiss her before they drank.

Holding hands, they finished the champagne, and he asked, "Do you really want scrambled eggs?"

Her breath caught as she met his glance, well aware of the meaning of his soft question. "No, Greg."

He came around to pull her chair back and, as she stood, picked her up, then carried her easily to their bedroom. Greg laid her on the bed, stretching her legs, and unbuttoned the top of her uniform pantsuit.

Four months pregnant, her flat stomach had changed, pouching a tiny bit over the flatness of before. Her small breasts were swollen and tender to Greg's touch.

"When are you going to wear maternity clothes?" he asked.

"Wait a couple of months and you'll say: 'You're getting too fat,'" she teased.

His hands caressed her cheek, tangling in her hair,

which she had unbraided. "Don't ever cut your hair or change the color of your eyes, Stacy."

"Brown eyes would go better with my hair." She frowned up at him.

He smoothed the frown away. "Never. They're the color of the jade plant, and you leave them that way or I may spank you."

She cuddled close to him. "Are you going to spank the baby if she's mischievous?"

"If he ever needs it, we will." His arms tightened and she forgot the discipline discussion as he whispered, "I want you." Mutual desire flamed and exploded between them, and he held her as she relaxed and slept in his arms.

Greg and the baby were the focal point of Stacy's world and she worked her classes and nursing duties around them. Final exams were due soon and she would have more free time for Greg.

Curled up on the built-in couch in their bedroom a few days after they moved into "The Place," she didn't hear Greg's car. She looked up to find him regarding her solemnly.

"Stacy, if you don't stop reading so much, you'll turn into a book one of these days."

"A few more days till exams, Greg. I plan to sleep a week afterward without opening a book."

"You worried?"

"A little."

He pulled her to her feet, said, "Come outside. I have your graduation present."

"A little premature, isn't it?" She lifted her face for his kiss.

Miracles Take Longer

His lips lingered on hers, then moved to kiss the tip of her nose. "I have faith in you."

He opened the heavy door, led her toward the driveway. Her eyes widened. A small green car sat sparkling in the late afternoon sunlight.

"Is it mine?" Her arms around his waist tightened.

For answer he held out a set of keys and said, "Look."

The back license plate read simply: STACY. She looked up at him, thinking only, *I love him too much.*

A few days later she parked the little green car in a reserved space behind the Broderick Building. She felt slightly light-headed as she waited for the elevator doors to slide open, then ran down the hallway when she reached Greg's floor, breathless with excitement.

Greta smiled at her from behind her always neat, efficient-looking desk. "Hello, Stacy. How's school?"

"Over," she said, and added, "Thank heavens. Is Greg in?"

Greta nodded, and Stacy was on her way, remembering the first time she walked down this hall. She knocked, heard a mumbled "Come in."

"Greg?"

He looked up at the voice, feeling the excitement in the small body. He studied her with serious blue eyes. "Are you playing hooky?" he asked.

She shook her head. "I've been to the doctor."

"And?" he asked.

"The baby moved. She's growing." She took a deep breath. "And, oh, yes, I passed my exams."

Greg sat watching her, saying nothing, until she realized he was letting her do all the talking.

"Is anything wrong?" she asked.

"Come here."

She went around the desk and he reached, pulling her onto his knees. His hands went under the overblouse she wore, touching the tightness of her stomach.

"He moved?" he emphasized, nuzzling her throat.

She looked into the blueness so close to hers. "We'd better have one of each, I guess."

"Why not?" He laughed against her mouth. "You passed your exams, huh? I don't have to ground you and take back the car?"

She failed to tell him she was first in her class.

WHEN SHE passed her sixth month of pregnancy, she handed in her resignation. She was tired from studying, keeping up with shift work, and trying to keep time free for Greg. The nursery was finished and she spent a lot of her time alone planning. She went to see Star and Rachel, recalling the murals Star had painted on the tent canvas, and the drawings in whitewash he had made in the red sand of the school compounds.

"Star, will you paint the nursery wall for me? I want a fairy tale picture, maybe 'The Cow Jumped over the Moon' in pastel yellows, greens, and maybe a tiny bit of lavender."

Star and Rachel were delighted that Stacy was having a baby, and no one seemed to care that she hadn't been married quite long enough for such a happening. Star considered her request, and nodded.

"I'm not sure I remember all the details, Stacy," he said, grinning. "Maybe the library in Phoenix will have a book to refresh my memory."

Stacy was sure she could depend on him to do a good job for her. Friends they still were, and she intended it to stay that way. Greg didn't want her going to the reservation often. He didn't openly disapprove, but he didn't trust Star completely, and discouraged her from spending too much time on the reservation.

"Let them be, Stacy," he cautioned. "They'll do all right without you."

"They are my friends, Greg," she said. "Do you want me to give them up?"

"No. Just be careful about staying too attached to them."

Greg left for San Francisco, and on his return she showed him the nursery, now done in the palest of yellows, Star's mural of the fairy tale covering one wall, every bit as delightful as she had known it would be. On the door she had placed a quilted likeness of "Happy," the irrepressible dwarf from Snow White.

Greg took it all in with obvious approval. "What about a baby bed?" he asked. "Can he sleep on the built-in one? Or will he fall off?"

She didn't correct his referral to a boy, telling him instead, "Rachel knows a lady with a large cradle. We can use that until he needs a bed."

He glanced at her. "He?"

She grinned. "Did I say he?" She shook her head. "Too quiet for a boy, Greg. They're never still."

Staying home all the time, Stacy loved the clean, spacious rooms of the house, protected from outside dirt and dust. She went from room to room studying the panels and grids expertly placed so they were hidden but energy efficient. Returning from her walks, which she took twice daily for her exercise, she stared in wonder at the home built by Greg's hands. Her first real home, a husband she adored, and soon a baby to share it. She hugged herself, happiness spreading itself throughout her body.

She went to Star with another plan. "Greg's birthday is October tenth. Can you do a painting of the house by then?"

"How big?" Star looked doubtful.

"I'd like it over our bed. About three by five feet. What do you think?"

Star thought about it a moment. "Maybe."

"How much would you charge for that?"

"I've never done anything like that, Stacy. I hate to charge you at all."

She shook her head. "I'll check on it and we'll agree on a price." They let it go at that.

It was late when she got home, and Greg was already there. "I was beginning to think I'd have to send a search party. Are we eating out?" He looked closely at the tired lines in her face, unusual in itself, because Stacy never seemed to tire.

"No, I have a roast. It'll only take a few minutes to finish it."

"Where've you been?" Greg took plates to the table.

"I went to the doctor, shopping, and to the reservation."

"No wonder you look tired. Don't overdo it, Stacy."

She smiled. "I really should do more. I'm getting fat and lazy."

Miracles Take Longer

As they finished eating Greg said, "I'll be going to Denver in a couple of weeks. Remember Oliver George, from Washington? He's meeting me there and we'll do some preliminary planning on those airport contracts he was interested in." He looked across at her, seeing that she hated for him to leave her. "If you feel good enough, would you like to come along on the trip?"

"Oh, yes, could I?" Green eyes grew bright with excitement. "I've never been to Denver, and I'd love to go with you. My appointment with Dr. Parks is next week, and I'll ask him about it, but I feel fine, so it shouldn't be any problem."

Still tired, she went to bed early, reading until Greg joined her. Drowsy and content, she moved closer to him, turning so she fitted within his arms.

"Too tired, Stacy?" he whispered against her hair.

For answer, she found his mouth with hers, loving his gentleness with her awkward body.

Uncomfortable if she stayed on her back for long periods, she turned to face Greg, her fingers trailing along his cheek, his throat, and to his chest, where she rubbed though the mat of curly hair. One finger moved across the flat nipple, and he tensed as she let the finger go on underneath his arm to pinch the hard flesh over his ribs.

He pulled her to him. "You know what?"

"What?"

One hand moved over her swollen abdomen. "He's beginning to come between us. Is this a preview of things to come?"

She laughed. "There's a remedy for things like that."

"Such as?"

She stretched her legs out and rolled over on her side, back to him, and wiggled until she nestled against him, one of his arms underneath her head, the other across her hip.

"How's this supposed to help?" he asked, his lips against her ear, his breathing already ragged as she pulled his hands to cup her breasts, moving his fingers back and forth across the swollen nipples. After a moment she moved his hands downward, pressing them into her thighs, opening them to spread his fingers around the tautness of her stomach. As his hands held her, there was a sharp movement from within and he tightened his hold.

"What was that?" he asked.

"That was your son, protesting, no doubt."

"Stacy." His voice was smothered against her shoulder, and he kept his hands still, waiting, but the movement wasn't repeated. "Doesn't that hurt you?"

"No, Greg." She drew her knees up, at the same time reaching to urge his hard thighs close to her. His response was immediate as he maneuvered her body, whispering words she didn't understand except for the tender sound, until his sudden gasp as he moaned, "Baby!"

She lay within the circle of his arms, a smile curving her mouth, even as she slept.

It could have been moments or hours later when she winced as she stretched her legs, trying to relieve the cramp that went from her thigh across the bottom of her stomach.

Greg was instantly awake. "What's wrong?"

"Just a cramp. I need to get up and move around."

He helped her up and rubbed her legs. "Feel better?"

"Yes." She took a step and cried out as the pain shot through her side. She felt the warm wetness on her legs, stared at the blood staining her gown. She saw Greg's white face, then darkness closed over her.

It was a tiny girl, as Stacy predicted, but she was too premature to live. It was odd that Greg found it harder to accept the miscarriage than she, but from experience Stacy knew it was better now than to risk a less than perfect, healthy baby at full term. Even so, for several days, she hit lows of depression, but she knew it was for the best, and Dr. Parks agreed with her.

"There's no reason you can't have other babies, Stacy. It was just one of nature's mistakes, and she corrected it as best she could." She saw the sympathy in his face.

"Yes, I know." She turned her face away from him, and waited for Greg to come to her.

Greg's eyes had dark circles under them. He sat, holding her hand, his voice hesitant as he asked, "Was it because of me, Stacy?"

She stared at him, not understanding. "What do you mean?"

He swallowed before he answered. "Maybe I shouldn't have made love to you."

Her denial was swift. "No, Greg. Any doctor will tell you that's the least of our worries. Don't you even think that, please. It would have happened anyway."

He smiled and squeezed her hand. "I was worried."

It was a week before she was allowed to go home, and Dr. Parks cautioned her against overexertion. Greg's grave attention to her every need built up her strength and emotions, and he hardly let her walk alone, much less overexert.

"You're going to have me very spoiled," she told him.

"Gotta get you back on your feet. I miss your getting under mine." He pulled a long braid as he passed her.

Mrs. Roper, who had been working for Greg for years at his apartment in town, came twice weekly to clean for Stacy, and she fixed stews and casseroles, putting them in the freezer so Stacy had only to take them out and reheat in the microwave oven, and Stacy considered her a priceless jewel.

She teased Greg. "Can I keep her even when I get over being lazy?"

"You can have anything you want, as long as I can have you," he told her, his hands exploring her still swollen body beneath the housecoat she wore.

"Greg." Her voice was just audible.

He pushed her away. "No, Stacy. You're tempting, but I know better. Soon, though." He kissed the top of her head and disappeared into his study.

Chapter Six

Each day, Stacy waited impatiently for Greg to come home, dreading the several days he would be in Denver on the trip he had postponed when she was in the hospital. She heard his car and went to open the door, a smile on her lips.

He didn't reach for her as usual, and she stared at him, seeing the dark, questioning gaze, his mouth a tightly closed line. She took a step backward as he looked at her.

He handed her a small piece of paper. "I want to know why you paid Star that much money."

It was her canceled check paying for the picture Star was painting for his birthday, a little more than two months away.

She opened her mouth to explain, remembered it was a surprise. Instead, she asked, "Where did you get that?"

"The bank put it in my statement by mistake. I'd like to know what it's for."

"You said the money was mine to spend as I wanted," she protested.

"Yes, Stacy, but within reason. I've never known you to spread money around so generously." His voice was cold. "If you planned to contribute that much to the reservation, I think I should have been told. I've been more than generous to them, I believe."

"But, Greg," she started.

"For what, Stacy? Tell me."

She was silent, feeling miserable.

"It's dated the day you had the miscarriage. Did you pay for an abortion?"

Her head jerked up, and she stared, openmouthed. When she managed to speak, her voice was barely a whisper. "You can't mean that." She shivered, watching his angry movements.

"What else would you spend a sum of money like that for? Did he use his Indian herbs and medicine man tactics on you?" He stood over her, his eyes glaring at her.

When she didn't answer, but stared at him in stunned silence, he grabbed her shoulders and shook her.

"Answer me, Stacy." His fingers bit into her flesh.

"If you love me, you can't believe I'd do anything like that."

He released her and said harshly, "Love wasn't in our bargain, was it?"

As he turned her loose she stumbled and sat on the window seat, seeing him through a haze of pain. The jade-green eyes reflected a puzzled question, changing to instant realization. Heavy lashes touched her cheeks and lifted to show the same green eyes with no expression at all. He thought they might be brighter, but wasn't sure, and he might as well have been looking at a painted wall for all he could read there.

Ignoring her look, he went on. "You made your plans well, didn't you? Get pregnant, refuse to have an abortion, very sweet, Stacy. I quote: 'I'll raise her myself.' When you made sure I was caught, you had an abortion so late it looked like a miscarriage. Nurses know about things like that, don't they? You were very quick to assure me that it wasn't my fault when I worried. At least, you didn't want me to feel unnecessarily guilty." Fury seethed in Greg like nothing she had ever seen as he condemned her, tearing her to pieces and not caring at all. "You were innocent sexually, I'll give you that, but you have a conniving little mind."

She didn't move, watching him. *That's odd,* she thought in surprise, *hearts really do break. I thought it was only a phrase.* Her hand went under her left ribs to press against the pain that threatened her breathing, and she was quiet as memories flashed past in rapid succession. A loan for medical supplies in return for her female favors. How could she have thought he loved her when she was only repaying a loan? They hadn't counted on pregnancy and a quick marriage.

I planned the pregnancy? A chill covered her entire body. Although Greg had done what he thought was right, he had never once mentioned love. She was the one who had fallen, so long ago it seemed she had loved him forever.

She glanced at the small rectangle of blue paper in

her hand. Just another computer error that switched a card from one slot to another, and ended her dream. For that was all it had ever been—a dream. A dream turned nightmare.

"I'll be at the apartment all weekend," Greg said, and she came back to the present to look up at him. She said nothing; there was no fight left in her. The door slammed behind him.

Stacy remembered little of the next two days as pain plowed through her body, physical in its intensity. She walked the floor of their bedroom, fighting nausea, and the only time she went in the kitchen was for a glass of cold orange juice to make it easier to swallow.

Greg called her on Sunday. "I'll be leaving for Denver Tuesday night. When do you go for your checkup?"

"Friday."

He hesitated a moment, then asked, "Do you need anything?"

Yes, she wanted to say, I need you. Aloud she said, "No."

He came at noon Tuesday, finding her on the window seat, one of his books open on her lap. It was the first time she had put on her jeans since she came from the hospital, and she wore a loose white blouse over them. Her hair was braided in big thick plaits, lying on her shoulders, a dark frame for a pale face with green eyes too big for it, lavender-tinted circles making them seem darker.

He looked at her, no expression on his face. "What time is your appointment Friday?"

"At two."

"I'll be back in time to go with you."

"Why?"

He smiled down at her. "I want to find out how soon we can have a baby." His eyes narrowed. "You do want a baby, don't you, Stacy?" His voice was dangerously soft.

"Without love?" she blurted out.

"You don't need love, Stacy. Just emotion." He stood over her. "Maybe I won't wait till Friday." He pulled her up into his arms, his mouth punishing and hard on hers, his desire to hurt her evident in the brutal force of his kiss, but she didn't fight. Holding on to his arms, she tried not to respond, feeling the love for him that he didn't want. He lifted his head, his breathing the only sound in the room, turning to put her on the bed, his fingers ripping the buttons from her blouse, pushing the bra straps aside. His lips closed on the small, firm breasts, just beginning to lose the swollen soreness from her pregnancy.

She didn't know if she made a noise, or if he realized what he was doing, but he pulled away, looking into her expressionless green eyes. With a muttered oath, he stood up, whirled, and stalked into the closet, pulling out his suitcase and the wardrobe hanger for his suits.

"Is Greta going with you?" she asked.

"Of course."

"I want to go, Greg," she said.

He turned, looking her over from head to foot. "What earthly good would you be on a trip like this, Stacy?" he asked bluntly.

She sat on the edge of the bed, hands holding the

front of her blouse together where he had ripped it. "Greg, about the money," she began.

"I'm not interested, Stacy. You spent it; we'll forget it." He went on packing, without looking at her. As he picked up his luggage he turned to look at her, his eyes still dark with rage, and said, "I'll see you Friday."

Curled up in the middle of the big bed, she heard his car pull out of the driveway. His plane would leave at seven and he would call her from Denver after nine o'clock. Or, perhaps, this time, he wouldn't bother.

What possible use could you be, Stacy? What use, indeed? There was no love in our bargain... no love in our bargain.... The refrain beat at her temples, starting a thundering ache in her head that swept through her slim body.

She watched the clock till it passed seven when she knew Greg's plane would be gone, then went into her own closet, looking at the few clothes she had collected. She was far from a clothes horse, and didn't spend money on things she didn't need. All feeling had disappeared, and she moved mechanically to do what had to be done, dropping the torn blouse into the wastebasket as she passed it.

The old blue suitcase was there, still holding her well-worn nurse's oxfords, and a bottle of polish. She took four uniforms from the drawer, wrapped in tissue paper the way she had left them, found her résumé with all her letters of recommendation, her Master's degree and credits she had collected, and placed them underneath the uniforms. They were in her maiden name, a plus for her, at least. She pulled out the faded all-weather coat and looked it over. The cashmere Greg had insisted she have would be out of place with the rest of her wardrobe, and she left it hanging in the closet with her few maternity clothes and the beautiful wedding dress, never worn since that fateful day.

She was back in the middle of the big bed when the phone rang at nine thirty. She let it ring three times before she picked up the receiver.

"Fields," she said.

"Stacy?" Greg sounded close enough to be next door.

Of course, it's me, she thought irritably. *Whom did you expect?* "Yes," she said aloud.

"Are you all right?" he asked.

"Yes." *What would you say if I said no?* she wondered.

"We'll be leaving here early in the morning, so I may not get a chance to call again." When she said nothing, he went on. "I'll see you at Dr. Parks's office Friday."

As the call was disconnected she stared at the ceiling, wondering how long Greg would have gone on letting her live in her dream world if she hadn't made the mistake of having Star paint the picture of the house for his birthday. Suppose I had told him what the money was for? What if the baby had lived? Would I ever have found out he didn't love me? Shudders shook her body as she tried to accept her own unrealistic attitude. *You are not naive, Stacy, you've been around long enough to see a storm coming before it hits you.* Where Greg was concerned, she had seen nothing since the day they married. There had never been any recriminations about her getting pregnant, and he had been the one who said they should marry. From then on, she had never thought of Greg any other way but loving her as she did him, although neither of them ever put it into so many words. *Dumb in capital letters, Stacy. I should have known better,* she whispered to herself. *Yes, I should have, but I didn't. I do now. Greg made sure I was aware of how dumb I was—am. Only time will tell if I've learned anything.*

It was only fitting that she suffer in the same room she had known such happiness in. Belonging to Greg for eight months was five more than she had bargained for, so she shouldn't complain. The fact that he had not loved her was no fault of his. He hadn't promised her love; only to be a father to the baby, and now that there was no baby to consider, he owed her nothing.

She went into the bathroom, taking the scissors with her. When she finished, the short hair curled in a feathered layer around her face, not much longer than the thick curved bangs. She placed the long braids in her suitcase. If anyone was looking for her, short hair would not be part of her description. *I really should leave them for Greg,* she thought. *My hair's the only thing about me he loved.*

I'll leave my eyes the same color for now, she thought, wishing she could spit the bitter taste out of her mouth.

She forced herself to return to thinking as Stacy Waring would think, a method of survival she had always practiced. One-hundred-and-eighty-degree turnaround from Stacy Fields. Her plans would have to be made as if she expected to be traced for some reason; as though someone might look for her; as if Greg might want her back. Her lips twisted to match the squeezing inside of her.

It hurt. The pain refused to lessen even as she pointed out to herself how ridiculous she had been to fall in love with a mortgage company. For that's what she had done—mortgaged her body to Greg for services rendered. *All right. Let's see what can be done to rectify my mistakes.*

Where would be the place to go from here? The farther from Arizona the better. Alaska. Sure. Greg would never look for her in Alaska. Her passionate dislike of cold weather was well known to him. The times when the winds blew through the desert and she curled against his body seeking warmth as she remembered the uncomfortable nights on the reservation when she slept fully dressed to keep from freezing.

In Greg's office she stood in front of a United States map he had on the wall. Arizona sits here and Alaska— what about Anchorage?—is all the way across the Yukon Territory from Seattle. That was far enough for starters. Maybe someday she could go on across Russia to Japan or China. Why not? Her fingers traced an imaginary route from Phoenix to Salt Lake City to Seattle to Anchorage, and the space between was no more vast than the emptiness inside of her.

Early Wednesday morning when the bank opened, she made her withdrawal and bought traveler's checks.

Driving by the bus station, she placed the suitcase she had packed the night before in a locker, checked schedules, and bought a one-way ticket to Salt Lake City, returning home to complete her plans.

She sat in the little car, gazing at the place she had called home for seven months, after a deliriously happy month in Greg's apartment following their marriage. Eight months total of heaven on earth—all she was to be allowed. With Greg free of his obligation, there was no reason for her to remain, unwanted and unneeded. He could use "The Place" as an example of the outstanding work he had done toward solar energy and conservation, impressing people like Oliver George who could be instrumental in bringing more fame and fortune to him.

Shrugging, glad of the cold numbness to keep her going, she got out of the car, standing for a moment with her hand on it, feeling the warmth of the motor, and went into the house.

From the small built-in desk in the kitchen, she took one of Greg's yellow legal-size pads. Her first note was to Star and Rachel:

> Our marriage didn't work. Give Greg the painting if he'll have it. If not, please keep it for me. I won't be in touch for a while, but will be thinking of you.
>
> Love, Stacy.

The second note was harder. She wrote a long letter, then tore it up. No need for detail; this one she could keep simple.

Greg:

Perhaps the ring will repay the money I used from your account. The amount I withdrew today will be paid back with interest as soon as I am able. Whatever you do about annulment or divorce is all right with me. I'm sorry.

Stacy.

It was amazing how much weight you could lose without trying; just forget to eat. The ring came off her finger with a slight twist, leaving a cold, bare space and a lighter circle to show where it had been. That too would fade, she thought, staring at the sparkling circle of diamonds before she placed it on the note along with her key to the house.

She went into Greg's study, passing the familiar desk she could almost see him bent over, going to the scrapbook that held pictures of many of the awards he had been given. Flipping through the pages, she found a clear photo of Greg and Greta that she pulled from beneath the plastic cover, then replaced the book on the shelf as she found it. She had grown fond of Greta, finding a sensible, fun-loving person behind the efficient secretary who had somewhat frightened her. Constantly with Stubbs when Stacy saw her, she seemed not to resent Stacy's marriage to Greg, even appeared to be happy for them. Perhaps she was a good actress too, Stacy thought. The picture fit behind the copy of her birth certificate in her billfold.

Down the hall at the nursery she stood a moment by the closed door, looking at the adorable likeness of

Happy, and turned away. *Well, Stacy, you bargained your soul and you lost. At least, the Indians got a little benefit from it.*

She would have to drive her car to at least walking distance of the bus station, and needed a way to have it returned to Greg. She must leave him everything that belonged to him, except one slightly used heart.

She drove into the service station where she usually bought gas. "Will you change the oil for me, Buddy?" she asked the young man who came toward her, smiling.

"Sure, Mrs. Fields," he assured her.

"And will you deliver it home for me?"

"Sure thing." He whistled as he got into the car to drive it into the work bay. One glance at the license plate that read STACY, and she left without looking back.

It was a short walk to the bus station. Dropping the note to Star and Rachel in the lobby mailbox, she retrieved her suitcase from the locker and checked it through with her ticket. She knew a moment of sheer panic as she thought of what she faced, all alone. *But I've always been alone,* she argued to herself. *What's the difference now?* Greg, a small voice inside her cried.

She remembered nothing of the long ride to Salt Lake City, and numb with exhaustion, she checked into a hotel close to the bus station and immediately slept. It had been days since she had slept more than fitful little naps and her body cried out for rest.

At the time of her appointment with Dr. Parks on Friday, she boarded a plane for Seattle, and Saturday she caught a flight for Anchorage. She had only a confused impression of land, noise, and water as she left behind all but Greg's memory, aiming for oblivion in the vast expanses of Alaska. Of all the places on earth, Alaska should be the farthest from Greg's mind to look for her if he felt any inclination at all. The biggest, geographically, of all fifty states, Alaska should be an ideal place to disappear.

Anchorage, in September, was hot and humid. Stacy blamed her extreme tiredness on the heat, knowing she had to get settled and see a doctor soon. Already late for her six-week checkup, she was aware that she didn't feel as well as she should at this stage of the game. Even so, she didn't leave the motel for two days, too tired to make the effort to look for an apartment or a job.

Stacy caught the bus that the motel clerk told her went past the main part of the city, and got off in a thickly populated area. Country girl gone to town, she thought, craning her neck. Anchorage wasn't what she expected.

With a population of only about a third of that boasted by Phoenix, it sat on a high bluff overlooking a branch of Cook Inlet, not much more than a hundred feet above sea level. A leaflet she picked up at the airport said it was Alaska's largest and most sophisticated city, the transportation and business center of the western part of Alaska, as well as a major winter sports center. She'd take their word for it. All her interests lay in finding a job and a place to live, and picking up the pieces of the mess she had made of things.

It was Thursday before she took her résumés and made her rounds of the hospitals, finding them as modern as everything else in Anchorage. At the second hospital where she placed an application, she was welcomed with open arms. June Whiting, Superintendent of Nurses, smiled at her. "You've no idea how much we need nurses with your experience. The high cost of living here drives most of them to go with the big companies, and I don't blame them." She sighed. "When can you start?"

"Monday," Stacy told her with relief. She gave only the Veterans Administration Hospital and Philadelphia General as references, not wanting anyone checking into Phoenix, perhaps providing an idea as to where she was. If anyone were interested.

There was plenty of room in the nurses' dormitory, for which she was grateful. Her meager belongings put away, she reported to the medical clinic. Checkups were free. *You would appreciate my being so frugal, Greg,* she thought.

The doctor sat down to talk to her after his examination, taking in her ringless fingers and the dark circled green eyes. "How long since your miscarriage, Stacy?" he asked.

"Eight weeks."

"You're a nurse. You know better." He frowned at the papers he held.

"Yes, sir." She waited.

He studied her chart. "Your blood count is low, and you have a slight kidney infection we can treat with antibiotics. I want you back in four days." He looked up at her. "I mean four days, Stacy."

Miracles Take Longer

She smiled. "I'll be here."

The antibiotics worked, and she began to feel better physically, but the cold emptiness lingered despite the hot temperatures. She settled into her routine, her twenty-seventh birthday came and went, with bare recognition from her. *Well,* she thought, *here I am at square one again. Just me against the same old world that hasn't changed much. But I have.*

After a month she began accepting overtime, two hours a day, and from there she went to six days a week. The hospital had great need for her services, and she had no use for time off to think of things best forgotten. The excellent salary, plus a cost-of-living wage that was added, dormitory living, and eating in the hospital cafeteria made it possible to save extra to apply to the debt she owed Greg. It was all very convenient, cold and calculated, and that was the way she would keep it.

On October ninth, she worked a double shift to be sure she would sleep through Greg's birthday without thinking about him, wondering even so if Star had completed the painting of "The Place."

It was early November when the first big snow came. Stacy walked the few yards from the hospital to her room, leaving the eleven-till-seven in the morning shift, as the swirling flakes fell in beautiful simplicity. And deadly. Accidents would be plentiful. *I hope I get some sleep before they start.*

She stood in the cold, remembering the warm desert. She wondered how the other part of the world was doing. Did Mrs. Roper still keep the house spotless? Were tumbleweeds blowing all over the barrel cactus in the front yard? Did the Indians have enough penicillin for colds? *Heaven help them—I can't.*

The somber sky reflected the heaviness in her heart, and she had come to accept this as a permanent condition. There were her memory times when nothing kept her thoughts from Greg, and she gave into them, feeling the gentleness of his touch, the sweetness of his lovemaking. The memory of her rude and devastating awakening followed, her body twisting in protest, her mind searching for escape. She walked in the snow, hating the wetness that went to her bones, wishing the icy winds would freeze her into forgetfulness, easing the pain at least for a time.

During the Christmas and New Year's holidays, she doubled shifts whenever she could, working for nurses with families who needed to be with them. She turned down invitations, preferring not to intrude in family get-togethers. Time began to perform its healing ways, and the pain she felt settled to a dull ache, at least bearable, and she forgot Greg for hours at a stretch, congratulating herself with a wry smile.

When she took her physical at Phoenix Medical Center after leaving the Mati Reservation, she had weighed one hundred and five pounds. During her pregnancy she had only gained eight pounds and had no trouble losing it, getting back down to her normal weight before the end of the six weeks, even though her body had still shown some swelling. She weighed ninety-five pounds when she checked in at Skowron General to go to work for June Whiting. Back up to one hundred pounds now, she felt stronger than she had in a long time, exercising at the hospital gymna-

Miracles Take Longer 115

sium three times each week. She still battled the low blood problem, but extra vitamins seemed to keep her from being so tired all the time.

She started a journal on the work she did, the few activities she took part in, some of the local scenery, planning to mail it to Rachel and Star sometime in the future. Not now. They didn't need to know where she was yet.

In February the Anchorage Fur Rendezvous celebration was under way, and for the first time Stacy became interested in an activity going on outside the hospital grounds. The city was alive with excitement and crowded for the winter carnival and fur auction. She watched as the owners handled the beautiful animals getting ready for the competition in the Championship Dog Sled Races.

"Would you like to go, Stacy?" June asked her. "I can get tickets."

Stacy and June had become friends as Stacy showed herself to be dependable and willing to work not only her own shifts, but any others where June needed her. Now she eyed Stacy as she stood by the window, wondering at the deep emptiness in the girl's strange green eyes. Even when she smiled, the eyes remained unchanged, staring at scenes that held no joy for her.

"I have an apple-red gown just begging to be worn, and it would fit you, Stacy." she said. "How about going to the Saturday night shindig that celebrates the end of the festival? Dr. Clark and his wife asked me to go, and I don't want to be a fifth wheel, but I'll go if you will."

Stacy looked at her doubtfully. "I haven't danced in

years, June. I don't know." An empty gnawing inside told her to accept the invitation.

"It doesn't matter. Let's go. It'll be fun to get out and dress up. Heavens, I'll bet you'll be the belle of the ball."

June talked her into it, and at nine o'clock Saturday night, they arrived at the ballroom to celebrate the festival with the entire population of Anchorage, or so it seemed to Stacy. Dr. Clark and his wife, a petite blonde named Tess, introduced them to so many people, Stacy's head was whirling.

The gown she wore, as June had told her, was bright red, showing off her smooth skin that seemed to hold a perpetual light tan. The short dark hair curved over her ears and thick bangs shadowed her eyes. Her borrowed plumage did a lot for her. A tight bodice gave way to a billowing skirt that showed the tip of silver sandals. Outside the snow fell, but inside the brilliantly lit ballroom, there wasn't the slightest chill.

"I can't believe this is our Stacy," a deep voice said, and she turned to see Dr. Thomas, Chief Surgeon at Skowron. "Who dragged you out?"

"June," she told him, smiling a little. "I'm going to play Cinderella and disappear at midnight."

"Oh, no," he said. "You can't do that." It seemed to break the ice for her and she was whirled from one pair of arms to another till she called a halt.

"I'm going home, June. You stay, and I'll catch a cab."

June laughed. "I'm ready too. Come on." They said good-bye amid protests and went to June's apartment for coffee.

"It was fun, June. Thanks," Stacy told her.

"How many dates did you turn down?" June asked.

Stacy laughed. "None."

"Nonsense. I know better." She looked straight at Stacy, sobering. "He must have hurt you really bad to turn you into such an indifferent person."

Stacy stiffened, feeling the blood drain from her face. Several seconds passed, and she looked up at June to say softly, "Yes. He did." She made no further explanation and June let the subject drop.

It wasn't quite true that there had been no invitations. Dr. Thomas had invited her to his dude ranch in Wyoming during spring roundup.

"You can ride a horse, can't you, Stacy?" he had asked, pale blue eyes going over her slim figure exposed in the red gown where he had always seen it covered in the puritan white of a nurse's uniform.

"Yes, I can ride," she replied, averting her face as the image of Greg laughing back at her as they rode on the Mati came to mind.

"How about an all-expenses-paid grand vacation in the wilds of Wyoming? Guaranteed to bring roses to your cheeks." Dr. Thomas was divorced, well known among the popular nurses, but Stacy laughed his invitation away.

"Thanks, but I've already planned my vacation and June will strangle me if I change now." She didn't add that when she went on vacation from Skowron, she wouldn't be coming back. By the end of June, there would be enough in her savings to pay off her monetary obligation to Greg, plus enough to see her through till she could find another job.

On Monday afternoon after the dance, Stacy stood in June's office, eyeing the snow-covered peaks of the distant Alaska Range, finding it hard to believe that a modern bustling city could sit so far into this cold wilderness. "When I leave here, I'm going to the Sahara," Stacy told her. "I haven't been warm since last summer." June hadn't questioned her anymore after her one statement, and Stacy volunteered nothing, seeing little to be gained by telling her story. She was not yet ready to tell her that she was planning to leave Anchorage in the summer.

In her journal to Star and Rachel she described the beauty and mystery around her. "It gives me an odd feeling to walk by the place they call Earthquake Park. At one time it was a rich neighborhood, but is now buried under tons of earth. To me, Alaska is a fierce enemy. Winters are rough, but in spring we look forward to floods, always a threat when the thaws begin, but somehow the people survive and love it. My first love is still the desert." She wasn't sure why she added that part. *Surely, my first and only love is Greg, no matter how hard I try to forget him.*

Wonder if he remembers our wedding anniversary? She refused to let her traitorous thoughts go any further.

Chapter Seven

Greg listened to the hum of the disconnected telephone call, replaced the receiver and tried to separate his thoughts. Stacy's voice sounded odd; she had answered yes to two questions, volunteering no information to him, and that was all. Uneasiness filled his body, and he paced the floor, restless and unsure of himself, remembering with disgust his last actions with Stacy. No matter what she had done, he had no right to treat her that way.

As the full realization of his accusations hit him, he drew in a sharp breath. Stacy could no more be guilty of an abortion than he could. *My God! What have I done to her?* He reached for the phone, then let his hand drop away. It was getting late, and she might be asleep. Stacy was an early person—early to bed and early to rise, as the old saying went, and since her miscarriage, she spent a lot of time resting, unlike the usual active Stacy.

I'd better wait till morning, he decided.

Leaving Greta, Stubbs, and Oliver in the restaurant after breakfast, Greg put in the call to Stacy, waiting impatiently as the phone rang. After the twelfth ring, he replaced the receiver, wondering where she'd be at seven in the morning. At nine o'clock he made the last call, then joined the rest of them going to the airport to check the area and equipment. He managed to stay until they had a firm commitment on the contract, then he gave in to his uneasy feeling.

"Take care of everything, Stubbs. I'm going home to see about Stacy," he told him Thursday afternoon.

The plane touched down at ten thirty Thursday night, and Greg waited with ill-concealed impatience for the baggage to be brought out. He couldn't wait to reach Stacy, to tell her he loved her more than anything, something he had just acknowledged to himself, and, whatever problem they had, they'd work it out. He was trying to think of words that would make amends for his accusations and gain her forgiveness. It was nearing midnight when he pulled into the garage, wondering why Stacy had left her car outside, but not wanting to take time to pull it inside. Later he would.

The garage door opened into the kitchen, and leaving his bags in the car, he started toward their bedroom, flipping the light switch on his way. The sheet of paper on the counter caught his eyes, and he stopped in midstride, a cold wind hitting his chest. He stood still, his attention riveted on the single house key and a sparkling circle of diamonds, lying on a piece of yellow paper. He pushed the items aside, leaning to read the note.

He whirled. "Stacy!" His long legs took him down the hall to their open bedroom door. Their empty bed-

Miracles Take Longer   121

room. Her bathroom looked the same as always, towels and washcloths hung in neat, color-coordinated arrangements. He opened her closet, staring at the few clothes hanging there. The only item he missed was the faded all-weather coat she, for some unknown reason, had insisted on keeping. The expensive cashmere coat, her maternity clothes, and the wedding dress still hung there, but the old blue suitcase was no longer on the shelf above her clothes. He opened the bottom drawer of the built-in chest; her uniforms were gone. As he turned away, something in the wastebasket caught his eyes. He drew in his breath as he recognized the blouse he had torn as he vented his anger on her. He groaned with an anguish he had never known before.

He didn't go to bed, and at daylight, drove to the reservation. She would come home with him if he had to drag her. He didn't share the sympathy for the Indians that Stacy had, and though he had helped them, it was because she wanted it that way. He should have known the reservation was too obvious, but all he could think of was her friendship with Star and Rachel. There was nowhere else for her to go, especially before her six-week checkup, and she would have to see Dr. Parks today.

Star opened the door of the partially completed adobe building, staring at the stern-faced man who had knocked. "Good morning," he said, not inviting Greg in. He waited.

Greg's mouth was a straight, angry line. "Good morning. Is Stacy here?"

Star pushed the screen door open, coming outside

onto the roughly completed porch. "No. Why do you think she would be?" He folded his arms, reminding Greg of stereotyped pictures of savages defying the white man.

He ignored the question. "Do you know where she is?"

Before Star could answer, Rachel stepped out beside him. "What do you want from us?" Her low voice was tagged with ice, letting him know she was aware of his feelings toward them.

Greg stared at Rachel, trying to remember if he had ever heard her speak. Even during the hearing for Dr. Grove she always seemed to remain in Star's shadow.

"You're her friends. I thought she'd be here, or that you'd know where she went."

"Why did she leave?" Star asked. He didn't seem surprised that she was gone.

Greg's eyes narrowed. "We had a misunderstanding," he began.

Rachel moved in front of Star, her dark eyes full of anger she didn't try to hide. "Misunderstanding? Oh, no. It wasn't a misunderstanding. Stacy understood too well." She took a deep breath and plunged on, raking Greg with her accusations. "Remember us? You shrug away our problems like so many insects. We're not forgotten Fathers of our Country. We're mothers. Abandoned mothers, left to welfare for survival. When Stacy left, so did our welfare. She always told me: 'Let's have our dreams first, Rachel; they're free. Miracles take longer, and we can't wait.'" Her anger swung to Star. "Show him the note from Stacy. Go ahead. It was Stacy's surprise for him, and she won't be back. No matter what blame he puts on us, let him see what she wanted for him." Liquid brown eyes flashed at Greg. "She didn't run away; you sent her away. Whatever you told her or did to her was the reason she left; not on her own. She loved you too much."

"Rachel!"

Star's quick exclamation didn't stop Rachel. Quiet by nature, she idolized Stacy, witnessing her struggle to make changes on the reservation that would help everyone, knowing Stacy had nothing to gain. Her voice was more calm, but she was determined to have her say.

"We don't know where Stacy is, and if we did, wouldn't tell you. If she left, she had a good reason, because you let her know she wasn't wanted."

Greg's own anger evaporated as he listened to Rachel's words cutting through him, knowing she was right. Too late, he remembered Stacy's eyes as he stood telling her there was no love in their bargain, green eyes that looked with absolute trust at him, changing to a glassy pattern without expression. Too late, he realized he had sent her away, the truth a knife twisting in his chest.

He read the note Star handed him. "What painting?" He listened, stunned, the accusations he had leveled at Stacy returning to haunt him. Perhaps she would have told him what the money was for if he hadn't told her he didn't love her, in so many words. If she did love him, as Rachel believed, and finding he didn't return that love, that he could accuse her of having an abortion, she would know there was nothing to salvage of the marriage, nothing to gain by telling him why she had spent the money.

He left the reservation, returning home to check just in case she came back, but he didn't really believe she would. He waited in Dr. Parks's office as two o'clock came, then two thirty, then three, but Stacy didn't keep her appointment.

Dr. Parks had no answers for him. "She's a healthy girl, Greg, but she needs medical attention now because of low blood, so common after miscarriages. I think Stacy will take care of herself." He added, sympathy in his voice, "I'm sorry."

Greg went to his office and sat way into the night, thinking of places she might go. She hadn't taken enough money from her account to last long, unless she went to work very soon. Was she physically able? She didn't go to Dr. Parks for her six-week checkup, but Stacy was a stickler about her health, knowing what neglect could do, so whom would she go to? Would she call him? *No, I'm sure she won't,* he thought, dropping his head into his hands.

Images came to mind and he saw Stacy's green eyes, sparkling with anger when he criticized the Indians. The night before they married, the uncertainty in her, as he showed her the ring. The night she had shown him how to love her when her body was big with his child. He had never doubted the baby belonged to him, because he had taught Stacy to love, had fulfilled her desire as she had him. Other women for him faded into non-existence after Stacy, and he had never been able to understand how one little girl could wipe out the memories of all other women.

Miracles Take Longer

There had been many, but he gave them up without regret. Stacy was winner-take-all, and he had lost her.

He stayed near the telephone all weekend, waiting, already knowing she wasn't going to call. He could feel the hurt that must have sent her away, knew almost exactly the way her small chin went up as she took on the world again without him.

On Monday he went to Phoenix Medical Center, talking to Phyllis Dorn about Stacy. "No, Mr. Fields, she hasn't applied to come back. If she did, we'd be glad to have her. We need more nurses like Stacy." He left, with the assurance that, if Stacy did apply for her old job, she would call him.

Greg made two calls that evening. One to Art Gordon in San Francisco; another to John Carroll in Dallas. Both were private detectives, two of the best in the business.

He had one alternative—work. As the days passed he stopped looking for Stacy each time the door opened, and buried himself in work he had always loved, but which now became a lifesaver. The book he was working on had been put aside during the time Stacy was in the hospital, while he spent extra hours with her, but now he went back to it, concentrating on research to keep his mind occupied. Nights were bad, and he spent most of them in the office, going to "The Place" only occasionally to check on everything.

Returning to the reservation time and again to see Star and Rachel, his greeting was cool, but he was doggedly determined that, if Stacy contacted them, he would know. Because of his feelings toward the

Indians, she had seen them less and less, but he knew they were as near to close friends as Stacy would ever have.

"She won't write until she gets over you," Star told him. "That may be never."

Greg stood with him outside the rough adobe walls Star was making into a home for him and Rachel. An amateur when it came to building, Star had some good ideas. He made up his mind, and said, "Look, Star, I can make some suggestions and help you with the house if you'll let me. It won't cost anything, and I'd like to do it."

"Why?" Star's question was quick and flat.

Greg shrugged, then grinned. "Stacy would want me to."

Rachel wanted no part of his help, but between the two of them, they convinced her, and it wasn't long before Greg was no longer a curiosity to the reservation, but a regular visitor. On his birthday Rachel baked a cake for him, and they presented the painting.

Greg stood looking at his home come to life on canvas, figuring the price was tremendous. It had, inadvertently, cost him Stacy.

"You painted it for Stacy, didn't you?" he asked finally.

Star regarded the finished product of Stacy's wish for Greg, and admitted, "I guess so."

The painting hung over the king-size bed in the place Stacy had selected, Greg stayed away from the bedroom, spending most of his time in the apartment, close to work, and miles away from Stacy's pride and joy, "The Place" that she loved.

Christmas came and went. Christmas Eve he gave a party for Greta and Stubbs, was best man at their wedding on Christmas Day, then saw them off on their honeymoon to Acapulco. The day after New Year's he flew to Washington to discuss airport plans with Oliver George. He watched the calendar pages turn until February 25, their first wedding anniversary.

Leaving work early, he went to the apartment, pouring his first drink at four o'clock. He spread a huge map of the United States on the carpet in his study, tracing all roads leading from Phoenix, and ending up where Art Gordon and John Carroll had—plenty of dead ends. By midnight he was drunk enough to sleep six hours, waking with a hangover like he'd never had before.

Stacy would say, "Serves you right," he thought, gazing at the bearded face and bleary eyes in the bathroom mirror.

And so began his second year of marriage.

"I wonder how you celebrated today, Stacy," he said aloud as he turned on stinging cold water in the shower.

Chapter Eight

The long winter months slipped into spring, warmer temperatures and heavy rains bringing the thaws that sent rivers and streams rushing over their banks, stranding people, leaving them homeless with just the clothes they were wearing. Stacy watched and worried, knowing some of the isolated homes were in plenty of danger, if not now, when the higher elevations got warmer and deep snows melted.

"What happens when all the roads get cut off, June?" she asked one day as they waited to cross a street downtown. They had been shopping and were on their way to June's car.

"Don't even think it, Stacy. It hasn't happened yet, but since the earthquake, some of the dams are weak and we live in horror of one of them going before their base can be reconstructed." June's hazel eyes searched the heavy clouds. Cottony edges on the darkness gave a metallic gleam to the sky. "The forecast is more heavy rains, and I don't know how much water this ground will hold, saturated as it is."

They put their packages in the trunk of the car, and

June pulled out into the early afternoon traffic. It was June's day off, and Stacy was due to go on duty at three thirty. She had bought Rachel and Star T-shirts with the Dog Sled Races on them. Someday she would mail them, perhaps put them in the same package as her journal.

When June dropped her off at the dormitory, she gave one more worried look at the sky, shaking her head. Coming from hot, dry Arizona to cold, mushy Alaska was as much a shock as from rags to riches. *Or do I remember what that was like?* She yanked her mind away from her past with its illusions and disillusions.

The rains continued unabated, and Stacy was assigned to an ambulance crew with Curt Dow and Roy Carson, patrolling the southern tip of the area that ran parallel to the peak of the lowest range of mountains to the northeast. In heavy pants and sweater, and boots that had become part of her life, it seemed, Stacy surveyed the rain-soaked lanes, leading into the more isolated areas.

The radio in the ambulance crackled as an emergency call came through. A family of three, including a tiny baby and the sick mother, were trapped in their cabin three miles from town in the heavily wooded area between two of the rampaging streams. As they approached the house from a narrow gravel road, Stacy stared in horror at the rushing water swirling around the house. They were perhaps a hundred feet from the house, edging toward the side where they could see a door, when the engine stopped, and the ambulance moved with the heavy current, drifting closer to the small building inch by inch.

"The rope, Curt," Roy yelled, wrestling with the steering wheel. "Get the rope around that post."

Together she and Curt pulled the rope around, struggling to stay on their feet. "It'll never reach," Curt told her, stretching as far as he could. The ambulance lurched forward, throwing him against the bench bed, and he lay stunned as Stacy held on to the rope and the door.

"I can't move my leg." Curt sucked in his breath as the pain hit him.

Stacy grasped the looped rope, trying to remember Star's instructions when he taught her to lasso along with the children on the reservation. "Get the heavy end nearest your body," he repeated to her over and over. Bracing against the door, her boot toe hooked around for safety, she swung her body out, letting go of the loop. It fell over the post, and her arms tightened as the rope lengthened. The ambulance tilted crazily as pressure from the rushing water forced it around.

Roy had left the driver's seat and crawled to check on Curt. "I'm okay," Curt told him, but his face was white. "Go help Stacy."

"I'll have to go across," Roy said, "and take a chance on that rope holding. Stacy, you hold the steering wheel, in case we come loose."

"The rope may not hold you, and you need to be here anyway. I can do it. Give me that life ring."

"No, Stacy," he protested.

She fastened the small life ring under her arms.

"Be sensible. You weigh two hundred pounds; I weigh one hundred," she told him. "Just hold on to everything from this end."

He knew she was right, but that didn't make him feel easier about it as he held one hand to balance her as she prepared to go through the ambulance door. Her slim body dropped into the water almost waist-deep on her, and both men watched as she went hand over hand with torturous slowness the few feet to the porch barely visible under the water. The force of the current pulled at her as she fought to keep her balance. She felt the boards beneath her feet, caught the post and pulled up till she could stand. Her boots were heavy, filled with water, but she didn't stop to take them off.

A man appeared at the door, staring in disbelief at the ambulance swinging at the end of the rope and the drenched figure a few feet away.

"Can your wife walk?" she asked.

He shook his head. By this time she had worked her way to his side. "Let me look." She glanced back at the ambulance, waved, and disappeared through the door.

Inside she had to wait a moment for her eyes to become accustomed to the semidarkness. Her heart sank, and she swallowed. *How in God's name will we ever get out of here?* was her first thought.

Furniture had been stacked to one side, forming a barricade in front of another door leading to the back. The dining room table had been pulled into the larger room she had entered, and a mattress placed on top. A young woman lay on it, pale, with large frightened dark eyes, watching Stacy's movements. A tiny blanket-wrapped bundle was held tightly to her breast. Water was over an inch deep on the floor, and rising.

Stacy's eyes took in the scene, and pushing the doubt to the back of her mind, she made her way to the woman and baby. The woman watched Stacy coming toward her with horror in her eyes, but Stacy smiled at her, patted her shoulder, and thought, *The baby made it this far; can't give up now.*

The man had stood by in silence, waiting. She turned to him. "Get that blanket over here."

His quick movements belied the huge frame. Stacy directed with few words and hand motions as they tied the woman and baby, backpack style, in the blanket. The man hooked it over his arm, and with Stacy lifting from behind, they made their way back to the post on the porch.

She stared, her heart sinking even lower. The rope would never hold the triple burden.

Roy cupped his hands to his mouth and yelled, "Stacy, there's a yoke on the wall." He pointed behind her.

Turning, she saw what he meant. A yoke used for oxen hung on the outside wall of the house. She took it down, made her way back to the shivering group, and handed it to the man.

"Fasten it over the rope, put your wife and baby in it, swing style."

The woman spoke for the first time, her face colorless. "No, no. My baby."

Stacy's voice was soothing. "I'm going with you. Just do as we say."

Miracles Take Longer

Together she and the husband fastened the blanket to the yoke, and Stacy slid into the icy water, turning to support them as he hooked it to the rope. Her arms ached as she held on to the precious burden. She looked back once. The man was holding on to the rope to steady it, eyes glassy with fear. She turned to the job at hand, taking a deep breath, forcing her numb legs to move.

Minutes later Roy pulled the woman and baby inside the ambulance. Stacy hung exhausted and half frozen on the rope, till Roy returned to haul her through the door.

"Can you swim?" Roy called across to the man. He nodded.

"Don't put all your weight on the rope, but use it to keep from drifting." In a few moments he too was pulled aboard.

"Now what?" Curt asked. He had pulled himself to a sitting position, the injured leg straight out in front of him.

Roy turned to the man who sat huddled with his arms around his wife and baby. "Cut the rope loose for me, and I'll try to guide us to higher ground."

With a reassuring murmur to his wife the man did as he was told. Stacy felt the ambulance vibrate, then inch away from the spot where it had been anchored by the rope. She heard a shout, saw a small boat headed their way, and men on solid ground. With chains and manpower they guided the ambulance to a relatively dry area.

The nightmare over, the little family taken care of by the hospital staff, Stacy sat in the coffee room, wrapped in warm blankets, a cup of hot tea in her hands. She took a swallow, trying to stop shaking.

"That was a dumb thing to do," Roy told her as he sat across from her chair by Curt, who had been X-rayed and sat with his foot propped on a stool.

Curt agreed. "Yes, sure was."

Green eyes surveyed them. "I can't imagine anyone being so dumb," she agreed.

Grinning, Curt said, "You were terrific, just terrific."

"Yeah," Roy said. "Remind me not to tell my wife I fell in love with you out there, stringy hair and all."

Good thing she didn't have the heavy braids, she thought. For a painful instant, she thought of Greg. It had been almost eight months since she left and no contact with her life in Arizona, her journal to Star and Rachel the only outlet for her feelings. Even so, she never mentioned Greg, or their marriage. It was as though it had never existed.

Maybe it didn't, she brooded. *A figment of my imagination; a dream that would fade from reality. If I'm lucky.*

Heroes were a dime a dozen during the flood crisis, and their effort went barely noticed, except by the hospital staff, who celebrated with a huge cake for them. Stacy forgot about it.

She had just finished her breakfast in the cafeteria when the announcement blared over the intercom: "Stacy Waring, please report to the Superintendent's office."

She groaned. *I'm too tired to work overtime, June. Go find someone else.*

But she put her tray up and headed for June Whiting's office.

"Good morning, Stacy." June smiled at her. "Do you remember anyone by the name of Joe Henderson?"

Stacy, who had the capacity to remember at least ninety-five percent of her patients, searched her memory, coming up with a blank. She frowned, shaking her head.

"He called, wanting to talk to you. I told him I'd ask."

"What about?" Stacy was still trying to remember the name.

"He said he's with Wilderness Radio," June said. "I've never heard of it."

"Neither have I. What do you think?"

"I'll call him back if you want me to."

"Okay." She grinned at June. "Why not?"

As Joe Henderson entered the room Stacy's recognition was instant. The man whose family they had rescued. What he wanted was an interview for his radio station.

Stacy spread her hands. "Why me? Curt and Roy did more than I."

The man smiled. "I was there, remember? I've already talked to Curt and Roy and have an appointment to tape an interview. I'd like you to appear on my morning show tomorrow.'

"You don't know what you're asking. I'll get up there and freeze."

He convinced her, and at eight the next morning

Stacy found herself before the microphone with Joe Henderson. She was shaking and told him, "It's a good thing it's radio and not TV. I can't be still."

He smiled at her, gave a signal, and she heard someone say, "You're on."

Joe began. "This is Wilderness Radio, and I have with me one of the many heroes of last month's rescue actions during the heavy floods. Along with two others, Curt Dow and Roy Carson, this young lady was instrumental in the rescue of my family. Meet Stacy Waring, a nurse assigned to an ambulance crew from Skowron General." He turned to Stacy.

"Stacy, all modesty aside, what makes people like you, Curt, and Roy, and hundreds of others, into heroes?"

She watched him a moment before replying. "Heroes? I've never looked up the definition of the word, Joe, but I'll tell you where to find them seven days a week." She saw his surprised look, but she went on. "Visit Skowron on Monday afternoon at two thirty, or Thursday morning at six o'clock, or Saturday night at eleven thirty. They're all there. Emptying bed pans, checking temperatures, holding a child, patting a hand." She took a deep breath. "Sure, it was a great effort, rescuing people from floods, and we're glad most of it was successful, but that's a one-time thing. To be a real hero you've got to be constant."

After his first start of surprise, Joe Henderson relaxed and let her talk, wishing she could be seen, the dark green eyes intense and sparkling, her hands moving with quiet expression. When she stopped, he smiled at her and spoke into the microphone.

"Some people don't recognize heroism when they see it every day, and Stacy Waring is a good example. A dark-haired heroine each day, but especially in emergencies. This is Joe Henderson of Wilderness Radio."

STUBBS APPROACHED Greg as he bent over plans he was studying. "Did you read the item a few weeks back about the floods in Alaska?"

Greg looked up, his mind still absorbing the plans. "Yes," he said. "It's that time of year again."

He hesitated, but Greg was looking at him, waiting for him to go on. "I was listening to the radio as I came from the dam, about three thousand feet elevation, and you know our radio skips."

"Yes?"

"Well, I heard—or I thought I heard—Stacy's name mentioned from a radio station somewhere in Alaska."

Greg stiffened and waited.

Stubbs was almost sorry he had started the conversation. Greg's eyes narrowed and went darker, his hand rumpling the plans he held.

"I didn't hear any area mentioned, but it sounded like an interview of some people who worked during the floods up there. The announcer said Stacy Waring." He stopped, his eyes riveted to Greg's face. "It might not have been our Stacy."

He and Greta had talked about Greg and Stacy, worrying over both, with no idea what they could do to help. When Greg and Stacy had married, they knew it was because of the baby, but as the months passed they saw love between them. Stacy had been as hard a worker as Greg, and her quiet sense of humor had balanced Greg's serious side. When she had lost the baby, Greg had been hurt too, gave her even more attention than before. Then, suddenly, she was gone, and Greg refused to talk about her at all, even though they knew private detectives were working around the clock to find her. She had disappeared without a trace.

Stubbs had gone on his own to talk to Star and Rachel, hoping something would suggest a clue to one of them. "We don't know where she is," Star had told him, and Stubbs realized he was telling the truth, seeing worry in the dark eyes. "We've heard nothing from her." Rachel had stood nearby, aloof as ever around strangers, but sadness was evident in her face.

He knew that Greg kept going back to the reservation, just to check, and after a time, he went almost every week, pitching in to help Star in building his house, and fixing up all the rickety huts he could into livable homes for the people Stacy had called her friends. He had finally recognized what Stacy had been trying to do, and why she had tried so hard to help, and Stubbs guessed it eased the ache inside him to be with others who loved her.

Stubbs came back to the present as Greg spoke. "Wasn't there any mention of a town or hospital?"

He shook his head. "I've been trying to separate all the words I heard clearly to come up with a name or a place, but all I caught was her name, and something about a family she helped save. I'm sorry, Greg."

Greg sat there, thinking of the huge state of Alaska.

Then he reached for the phone. "Greta, get me Art Gordon and John Carroll."

STACY SHRUGGED away any mention of the broadcast and handed in her resignation, effective in mid-July.

"Oh, no, Stacy, I was hoping you'd stay." June was dismayed. She had seen Stacy grow restless as the weather improved, and had tried to interest her in fishing and camping with other nurses and their families, but even though they had become friends, she couldn't get close enough to Stacy to question her about any family she had. According to her employment papers there was no family, but something or someone had hurt her. Even Stacy admitted the hurt, but that was all she ever got from her. There were no details.

Stacy only shook her head and June asked, "What are your plans?"

"I don't have any," Stacy said. "Except find a warmer climate before cold weather comes around again."

She had no real regrets at leaving. It had been a good job, good co-workers and experience, hard work to crowd out memories, and good pay to help her save more than she could have imagined.

At the bank an accountant figured the interest on the money she owed Greg. She mailed him a check for the amount along with the accountant's statement. As she filled in the blanks on the check, a curious ache filled her. Were checks always blue? she wondered, remembering that one that had gone to Greg's account in error. While she was at it, she wrote a smaller check for Star and Rachel, sure that they could always use it for something.

The journal she had been keeping for them was complete now, and she put all the year's activity recap into a stationery box, a small clipping about the flood and the radio broadcast, and the T-shirts she had bought, mailing them as one package. It no longer mattered that they would know where she was; by the time it arrived at the reservation, she would be on her way somewhere else. Not even she knew where she would be going.

Unable to sleep following her trip to the bank and Post Office, Stacy stood at the window, watching the northern lights as she had so many times, puzzled by the phenomenon no less now than the first time she saw it. The nights were so bright that her night shifts seemed little different from day duty.

Where will I be a year from now? she wondered, turning away from the outside spectacle. In her mind she searched the mainland states for a suitable place to relocate. The southwest appealed more to her, Arizona in particular, but that was out of the question. Although, come to think of it, she could probably work at Phoenix Medical and no one would know or care. She pushed the thought away. She certainly had no desire to return to the Philadelphia area. Houston and Dallas were too big. So were Atlanta and Miami. Las Cruces or El Paso? She shrugged. What did it matter, really?

She sat at the small, straight table that served as her desk, and pulled her notebook to her. Without thinking, she started writing.

Dear Greg:

A year has passed since last I saw you, and I guess you have seen changes as I have, some good, some not so good. There has been no change in my feelings for you as I had hoped there might be, and the love is still there, as deep as ever. I wish it wasn't true, but have ceased trying to fool myself, and I live with it as best I can.

She reread the lines, acknowledging the flat truth she had written. She went on with her thoughts.

We made the strangest bargain ever, I suppose, and it ended not too strangely, considering the circumstances. Your accusation that I had a "conniving little mind" still fascinates me, because I wished so many times that I had been able to hold you, anyway I could, fair means or foul; I would have considered them all. But my mind and heart were so clouded with love for you, I thought everything would be taken care of by that love. I have been wrong many times, before and afterward, but never so wrong as in my love for you. I still look for you in the evenings when things get a little quieter, and I'd love to talk to you the way we use to do. Some of those times, I must admit, I didn't hear a word you said; I was too busy watching you and loving you, treasuring every moment we spent together. I guess it was good I did that because our times together were limited.

She stopped again, then went on to tell him about her job and living conditions in Anchorage. She mentioned the rescue of Joe Henderson's family without going into details of her part in it. When her letter was completed, she had written ten pages, both sides. She read it over to see if she had left out anything of importance, tore it across once, then again, and threw it away. She smiled to herself as she pictured Greg's reaction if he received such a letter. Shock? Pity? Outrage, certainly. She had not been able to mention the baby.

It was late, but she pulled the old blue suitcase from the closet, placed it on the bed, and unsnapped the latch. Inside were the braids she had cut a year ago. She fingered the heavy braids, as shiny now as they were when she cut them, remembering her reason for the drastic measures she had taken. If Greg gave a description of her, no one would look for a small green-eyed girl with dark brown hair that lay in a feathery fringe against her cheek, barely covering her ears. She could have saved herself the trouble; no doubt, he had never looked for her. For a moment she felt a terrible loneliness. In the world with millions of people, not one cared that she existed.

She shook her head. Why brood? In a short time she had packed items she wanted to keep, and the rest she sorted into piles. The faithful old all-weather coat was falling apart and went into the garbage. Her best uniforms she put aside for June, in case someone came in who needed them. There was enough money now to replenish her wardrobe, and it could certainly stand it. Her few winter pants and skirts went to the

Salvation Army. When she finished, the suitcase held everything that was left.

It had been eight years since she bought that suitcase; she'd traveled thousands of miles and still hadn't collected more than enough stuff to fill it. It must be some kind of record, she thought. *You don't need space to pack memories. They follow whether you want them to or not.*

Ah, yes, memories, Stacy thought, closing her eyes. *Those things that haunt you forever.*

Chapter Nine

The airport in Seattle was crowded with summer vacationers. Collecting her bag, she walked toward the information booth, watching people talking, laughing, hugging. They knew where they were going, at least.

Detouring away from the booth, Stacy sat down against the wall where she could see the panels listing all the flights from Seattle, Chicago, Denver, Detroit, Los Angeles, Phoenix. Phoenix. Even the name brought back the terrible homesickness that had haunted her for months.

No, she thought. *I can't go back.* You can never go home again. Where had she heard that? And where was home?

An announcement came over the speakers. "Special discount rates now in effect for flights to Hawaii. Save up to forty percent over regular fares."

Now, there's a place where I'd probably never be cold, Stacy thought. She sat still, listening as the announcer went on with his spiel about the beauties and enticements of the lovely islands.

A few people lingered at the counter as she approached, some asking questions about the special rates.

"To get the forty-percent discount, you must travel Monday, Tuesday, or Wednesday, and stay at least ten days," the man said.

"What about a one-way ticket?" Stacy asked.

The young attendant eyed the girl before him, taking in the slender figure dressed in black pants, a black and white checked blouse with a black blazer over her arm, and a battered blue suitcase at her feet.

He smiled. "The same rate applies."

"Do you have any literature on the islands?" she asked.

"Sure." He turned to the counter behind him, selected several pamphlets, and gave them to her.

She went back to the seat against the wall and sorted through the material. For a long time she stared into space, seeing and hearing nothing, though activity surged around her.

I'd love to see Star and Rachel, she thought. *And Greg. And the house.* She wondered what he did with her car. Did he accept the painting? Did he get an annulment or divorce and marry Greta? *I don't even know if I'm still married. Not that it matters.* She shivered.

What earthly good would you be on a trip like this, Stacy?

Not much, she had to admit.

She waited until the attendant was free, then went back to the counter. "Do you have any reservations to Hawaii for today?" she asked.

He stared at her. "Do you have people over there?"

She shook her head.

"You're just going? Ever been there?"

"No." She smiled. "Is that a requirement?"

"No, of course not. But—" He stopped. "You look so young to just make up your mind and go. It's still a lot of money, even with the discount."

"Yes, I know it's a lot of money," she told him, ignoring the part about being so young. "You can choose any of the islands and still get the discount, right?"

He nodded.

"Would you check to see when you have a reservation for Hilo?" she asked. Hilo, a city of approximately thirty thousand people according to the pamphlets, was located on the island of Hawaii, largest of the island chain. Although having its share of visitors, Hawaii had less tourists than Oahu, where Honolulu, the capital city was situated. However, it was still well populated, which meant hospitals, which meant jobs for nurses. She could do without all those rich tourists, Stacy thought, and made her decision to go to Hilo.

"Just a moment." She watched as he punched the computer and waited. "There's a flight tomorrow morning that goes to Hilo, after a stop in Honolulu. It will put you there about noon, Hawaii time."

"I'll take it," she said.

She purchased her ticket and went into the coffee shop to order a sandwich. She let her thoughts ramble. *If I keep running, perhaps one day I'll run far enough to lose even the memories. At least, it doesn't hurt as much as it once did to think of Greg.* She smiled at her coffee cup. Who was she trying to fool?

Her breath caught as Greg's face suddenly came between her and the coffee cup. Smutty lashes framed the navy blue eyes, and a half smile curved his mouth. She squeezed her eyes shut, but his image stayed on her closed lids. It had been months since she allowed any thoughts of Greg to linger more than seconds, but somehow she couldn't rid herself of him. Again she felt his hands on her, heard him say, "Don't ever cut your hair, nor change the color of your eyes."

"Are you all right, ma'am?"

She opened her eyes to see the young girl who had served her sandwich staring at her with concerned eyes. She blinked. Greg had disappeared, but the sound of his voice echoed in her mind.

"Yes, thank you. May I have my check?"

She paid her check and asked for what was due back from the ten-dollar bill to be given her in change. She could at least hear Greg's voice once more before she left the mainland for good.

Taking the several dollars in change the cashier gave her, she went into a phone booth. Dialing 0 for long distance, she explained, "I want to call a Phoenix, Arizona, number, but the call is to be a surprise. Could you please allow me to deposit the money without disclosing the origin of the call?"

"Of course, ma'am. Let me give you the charges for the first three minutes. You'll speak with anyone who answers?"

"Yes," Stacy said, rubbing her sweating palms against her pants leg. It was eight at night. If anyone answered, it would be Greg. Surely, Greta would be at home, or out on a date, even with Greg, for that matter.

The operator came back on the line. "That will be two dollars and seventy-five cents for your first three minutes."

Stacy listened to the coins rattling into the slot and a split second later the phone rang in Greg's office. It rang four times, and with a sigh of almost relief Stacy started to replace the receiver, when, in midring, the phone was picked up, and Greg's voice, vibrant and deep, came through.

"Greg Fields."

Her heart pounded until she was sure he could hear it, and she held her breath, as he spoke impatiently into the phone. "Hello? Hello?"

Stacy placed the receiver carefully back on the hook, knowing Greg would mark it down as a crank call or someone who got a wrong number and wasn't polite enough to say excuse me.

So he still stays late at night, absorbed in his work. I guess he hasn't changed since I left. Why should he? I was an interval best forgotten. She knew she would be sorry, but Stacy had to hear his voice, after a year of silence. She left the phone booth, thinking, *I should have said, "Hello, how are you?" anyway.*

GREG HELD the phone in his hand after he heard the receiver replaced on the other end of the call, a curious tingling in his body. There had been no sound on the phone, not breathing or static you sometimes get on a short-circuited call. He put the receiver back to his ear, hearing only the dial tone, but he stood there, feeling Stacy's mouth against his. Perhaps she was thinking of him, wherever she was. His mouth twisted as he recalled that he was the one who had sent her away. He turned, going back to the table where he had a set of plans spread, but he didn't see them. Restless now, he switched off the lights and left the office, finding himself in his car, headed toward "The Place." He didn't stay there much since Stacy left. For a man who had never been lonely, the house was unbearable without her, and he was always looking for her when he was there. He never opened the nursery door, depending on Mrs. Roper to dust every few weeks.

He walked through the house to the bedroom, looking a long time at the painting over the bed, and back to his study, stopping to pour himself a small bourbon and water. He pulled one of the scrapbooks from the shelf, turning the pages without seeing the pictures and articles. Stacy used to spend hours going over his collection of awards, asking questions about what he had done to get them, fascinated by his work. His hand touched a spot near the center of a page, a small blank area, as though something had been removed, but he couldn't remember what should be there, if anything. He sighed, stretching his long legs out in front of him, staring at the bookshelves loaded with his success story.

If Stacy were here to share it, he thought, for perhaps the millionth time, and wondered as he did every day, where she was, and if she was all right. For a brief interval he held hope after Stubbs heard her name on the radio, but if that was Stacy, she was just as elusive as ever.

The morning's mail brought the check from a bank in Anchorage, Alaska.

STACY SPENT her last night in Seattle at a nearby motel, sitting for a long time at the window, gazing at the lights, listening to the noises of the big city. The noise seemed much worse than in Anchorage. The snow acts as insulation, she thought.

She slept most of the ay to Honolulu. The bright, clear atmosphere, and the blue of the sky combined to make her lids heavy, and she was glad to lose consciousness.

The captain made the announcement as they approached the island of Oahu. "Ladies and gentlemen, we're coming into Honolulu, one of the loveliest cities in the world. We will be staying here for an hour, before continuing on to Hilo, a forty-five-minute flight. Passengers may leave the plane. Please place a reserved card in your seat as you leave. Thank you."

Stacy didn't get off the plane, but watched with interest as the beautiful Hawaiian girls presented the legendary orchid leis and a kiss to passengers departing the flight. Wearing long, colorful dresses wrapped around their slim, suntanned bodies, they swayed in graceful accompaniment to Hawaiian guitars and ukuleles.

If Hilo is anything like this, I'll love it, she thought.

Imagine dressing like that all year and no snow. She smiled.

She fought sleep on the short flight to Hilo and came wide awake as they landed and she could see festive crowds waiting for them. There weren't as many people as had been at the airport in Honolulu, but they were greeted with the traditional flowers and songs, and Stacy gazed around her in disbelief. She slipped away from the crowd, found a taxi, and went into the city.

"Is there a small motel I might get a room?" she asked the driver.

"The Island Hotel is small and it's off the beaten track," he told her. "Is this your first trip here?"

"Yes."

He grinned over his shoulder. "Where you from?"

"Alaska."

He whistled. "Boy, when you change, you really change." She agreed.

The hotel was small, clean, and there was a vacancy. She put her suitcase down, walked through the room and bath once, and went out to roam the streets.

Hours later she returned to the hotel, tired and strangely content. All the color brochures she had read had not done a creditable job on their tributes to the beauty of Hawaii. Or perhaps they've never seen all the ice and snow in Alaska, nor the dreary desert in Arizona. Her heart tripped, and she went to wash her face.

It was late when she awoke the next morning, and Stacy was lost for a few moments as she gazed at the brightness in her room. Her body still heavy with sleep, she slid from the bed and went to the wide windows overlooking the yards below her. She pushed the draperies aside, peeking out at a world that was a kaleidoscope of rioting color, and she drew in her breath.

This view would take some getting used to. From the Arizona desert, to Alaska, to the Hawaiian Islands. *You've come far, my girl, but not quite far enough. You still remember Greg. And, he, after all, is your reason for running.*

Resolutely, she dressed in the black pants she had worn on her flight, but found a short-sleeved white blouse to go with it instead of the black-and-white checked long-sleeved one she had used for traveling. Skipping breakfast, she headed for the downtown area where she could look in some store windows.

She had walked almost two hours, breathing the pleasant air, watching people saunter by, lots of them tourists, she knew by their clothing. She bought one pair of green shorts with a green and white striped knit shirt to go with them, and black thong sandals.

As she left the department store she saw a small restaurant and went in search of food. Hungry all of a sudden, she ordered a huge fresh fruit salad and coffee. Her table was on an open veranda facing the beach and she dawdled, her eyes going from people to beach to pounding surf, a shade of blue she had never seen until now. By the time she finished eating, she was so sleepy, her eyes kept closing. She took the hint, returned to her room, and was soon fast asleep.

A strange sound awakened her and she lay still, listening. Rain? She rose slowly, looking around the still strange room, and went to the window to pull the draperies. It was pouring rain, and she gazed, mystified, at the sudden change from sun to hard rain. Even as she watched, the rain diminished, the clouds parted, and the sun came through.

She smiled, hugging herself. The sudden showers had been mentioned in one of the brochures she had read. And after the showers, the sun was back in all its glory. The brochures did not exaggerate.

The next day she boarded one of the tour buses that made an eight-hour tour of Hilo and vicinity. They were going through a section of huge mansions their guide pointed out as belonging to various movie or television personalities and Stacy overheard an older lady comment to her companion, "Can you believe people have enough money to pay two million dollars for a home they live in three months of the year?"

Stacy agreed, eyes wide, trying to absorb the wild, lush beauty of her new home. Star and Rachel would never believe it, she thought, and a deep sadness intruded in the bright afternoon. She shrugged it away. Hawaii was a good move for her, and though she had a lot to forget, she was sure this was as good as she could ever do.

Sleep that night came easy and early, and when she woke, she felt more rested than she had in months. She took the phone book and sat on the small patio outside her room. There were several hospitals on the Big Island, including a rehabilitation center she had seen as she toured the area. She took her résumé from the suitcase and leafed through it. Before leaving Anchorage, she had added her experience at

Skowron, plus her letter of recommendation and the write-up from Wilderness Radio.

Renting a car, she drove out to Grant Memorial Hospital on the outskirts of the city, one she had spotted as they toured. She parked in the visitors area and walked through the grounds where flowers grew in wild abundance of reds, yellows, and purples.

No wonder they called it Paradise, she thought.

How could states like this and Alaska be in the same country? she wondered, the difference so striking as to be ridiculous. Millions of people like snow, she admitted, but for her, it was just cold. And then, there was Arizona, another entity all to itself. *Maybe I'm the one who's too different to be accepted*, she thought, inclining her head in immediate acceptance of that fact.

In the entrance hallway she found a directory of offices and headed for the one marked Personnel.

The receptionist smiled as she stopped in front of her. "May I help you?"

"Yes. I'm Stacy Waring. I would like to apply for a job," she said.

"What are your qualifications, Miss Waring?"

"I'm a registered nurse with a Masters in Medical Science." Thanks to Greg's generosity. She had Greg to thank for a lot of things, including growing up. *If I have.*

"Just a moment, please." The young girl in front of her got up and walked to a closed door, knocked, then disappeared. In a few moments she was back.

"Miss Waring, Mrs. Bowden will see you in a moment. Do you have a résumé?"

Stacy handed her the papers and watched as she looked through them. The door to the other office opened and a middle-aged woman with silver hair walked toward her.

"Miss Waring, I'm Maureen Bowden. Come in, please." She took the papers from the receptionist and led the way back into her office.

"How did you end up here, Stacy?"

"Running from cold weather," Stacy said. *Among other things,* her heart finished for her.

Two days later she moved back into a nurses' dormitory. *One of these days, I'll have me a house,* she promised herself. *Until then, dormitories will have to do.*

Before reporting for duty, she had to shop for uniforms, replace the ones she had left for June to use. It had been a long time since she had been shopping for anything except her shorts set and she decided she'd take her time and enjoy it. She found the uniform shop first, bought two dresses and four pantsuits, and two pairs of nurses' oxfords, completing her shopping with all new underthings.

Packages under her arm, Stacy strolled down the street, stopping to look in the store windows at the colorful array of clothing. Everything was so bright; *exotic* was the word. She stood looking at the garments called muumuus, a sort of wear-anywhere-for-everything loose outfit the Hawaiians used for almost any occasion. She loved them. On impulse she went inside the store. Up close the colors were even more gorgeous, and she fingered one in cool blues and greens, not daring to look at the price. She didn't actually need to check the prices on anything, but old habits died hard, and she couldn't stop herself from thinking about how long it would be till payday. She had saved plenty while in Skowron, paid her debts, and could buy what she wanted.

"May I help you?"

Stacy turned at the soft question. A lovely girl, with Oriental features, stood smiling at her.

"I don't know how these are sized," she said, hesitating over the purchase. She had spent a lot of money, and her old thrifty nature was asserting itself.

"You would take a petite size, I'm sure. You can try it on in here."

The young girl smiled, her almond-shaped dark eyes approving. "That color would be very pretty with your eyes."

Don't ever change the color of your eyes, Stacy. She swallowed hard.

Once she saw the muumuu on, she couldn't resist it. Feeling deliciously sinful, she paid for it and left the store.

In her room she spread out her purchases, putting the uniforms aside to rinse out before she wore them. She counted the money in her billfold to see if she needed to cash a check before payday. Not likely. Hesitating, she slid her finger behind her birth certificate and removed the picture placed there a year ago. She had never looked at it since that time. Now, she stared at the faces from yesterday; the man she loved and perhaps the woman he loved. Both very nice people. She sighed, putting the picture back in the same place.

Stacy slipped back into the hospital routine as

though there had been no interruption. It seemed peculiar that in such a beautiful place the same diseases and pain existed as anywhere else. She let her mind try to absorb what she couldn't change, and walked through the huge, modern building, becoming familiar with the layout so she wouldn't be confused her first tour of duty.

At Grant Memorial there were two things that bothered Stacy. People, rather. Number one was Dr. Mark Grant, whose grandfather had built the hospital, and whose money still paid most of the bills. Dark blond hair, tanned, over six feet tall, green-flecked brown eyes, and a firm mouth not given to smiling. Between thirty-five and forty years old, she guessed.

Dr. Grant was known as one of the best surgeons anywhere in the island chain, known for his skill and intelligence. Stacy gave him that, plus he was abrasive, demanding, and capable of harassment if he didn't get the response he wanted in record time.

Well, not really harassment, but make one wrong move and you got chewed and berated right then and there.

Stacy had been on the receiving end of his displeasure more than once, but she could turn him off even though working alongside him. Anna Boyd, on the other hand, took him seriously, intimidated by his brusqueness.

For some reason Anna decided Stacy was a solid wall for her to hide behind. Unsure of herself, her big brown eyes seeing the world as a machine ready to gobble her up, an irritating habit of beginning every other sentence with "you know," tempting Stacy more than once to say, "No, I don't know," Anna depended on Stacy to run interference for her.

Anna was a good nurse, and Stacy found it hard to believe she could be so unsure of herself as to need a front between her and Dr. Grant. She told her in no uncertain terms. "Fight for yourself, Anna. I won't be here forever to fight for you." This was after Dr. Grant had barked at her when she wasn't quite fast enough in handing him the instrument he requested. Stacy smoothed it over, and unobtrusively edged Anna out of the path of his venom. Dr. Grant didn't miss it and afterward told her.

"Let Boyd do her own corrections, Waring. That's how she'll remember next time."

"Yes, sir," she said, without turning.

She changed from her uniform to white linen slacks and navy blue T-shirt, went down the hall to Room 310, where her second problem lay. He was Danny Martin, a five-year-old with leukemia. The disease was in a state of remission now, but Stacy faced the fact each day that it was only a matter of time for it to flare up again.

Danny, sweet and lovable, liked having Stacy around, so she spent a lot of her spare time with him.

He opened his eyes as she touched his hand. "Hi, Stace," he said, shortening her name as he always did. "Tell me about the abomdable snowman."

She laughed down at him. "Sure, Danny. How about some orange juice first?"

"Okay." He wouldn't touch orange juice for anyone but her.

She was telling him her own version of the Abominable Snowman when she looked up to see Dr. Grant in the doorway.

Danny saw him too. "Stace is telling me a story, Dr. Grant." His voice was slow, and his eyes heavy, as he tried to stay awake.

Dr. Grant picked up the small hand, checked his pulse, touched his cheek, looking at Stacy as he smoothed the fair hair back from Danny's face.

"Aren't you off duty?" he asked.

"Yes, sir."

He looked back at Danny, whose eyes were closed. "How about some coffee?" he asked.

"No, thanks." She stood up to go. She got enough of him in the operating room without any other association with him. Besides, nurses and famous surgeons just did not socialize with each other.

"Why not?" he asked, staring down at her, the frown on his face telling her he didn't appreciate being turned down by anyone for anything.

"I have some work to do," she told him.

As she walked down the hall she was conscious of Dr. Grant's long legs beside her, and they waited in silence for the elevator.

On the first floor he said, "This will only take a few minutes." His hand on her elbow guided her through the cafeteria door.

She let him pay, saying only "Black" when his eyes questioned her. At the table she studied the face opposite her. Most of the time around him, she was on the defensive and never really saw him, even though the other nurses swooned over him when they weren't scared to death. The dark blond hair was thick and slightly waved away from his tanned face. The light brown eyes had green flecks that were darker now that she was so close to him. The thick dark lashes were stubby. Her eyes went to his mouth, which she saw mostly in a stern line when he was reading somebody the riot act. Right now it curved in a half-smile.

"Will I do?" he asked.

She lifted her glance to his, felt the color in her cheeks, but she said only, "Yes."

"Maureen tells me you came from Anchorage. Did you like living there?" He looked interested.

She didn't answer him at once but sat looking into her coffee cup. I didn't live there, she wanted to say. I existed. When she raised her eyes, Dr. Grant was watching her curiously.

"It was all right. The winters are rough, but I had a good job."

"Do you ski?"

She shook her head.

He went on. "Out here, it's water skiing and surfing. Lots of fun. You should take lessons."

"No, thanks," she told him. "I don't trust those big waves batting me around. I might end up in China, and I like it here."

He laughed. "You learn to ride with them, not fight them. The same as you do anything else."

She sensed an underlying message in that, but decided to ignore it.

Dr. Grant continued to look at her, and she sat still under his scrutiny, deciding he would let her know why he was buying her coffee when he got good and ready.

"Where do you live, Waring?" he asked, after his eyes had gone over her face several times.

"In the dorm."

He raised an eyebrow. "How are the facilities?"

"Austere." She smiled. "But adequate."

He leaned toward her, elbows on the table. "If you could, what would you change?"

She frowned at the question. "Why?"

"Just curious. You evidently have some ideas."

She thought for a moment of Greg's house: the thick, silent walls, the secure doors that no self-respecting thief would even dream of trying to open, the skylights she loved that let in all the brightness and no dirt. But to change dormitories to that type building would take Fort Knox.

She shook her head. "A little bigger, more privacy, more insulation so you could concentrate on studying, kitchenettes for full-timers, safety doors that open only from the inside on the lower floors."

"Whew! You do have some ideas."

She shrugged. "You asked." She pushed away her empty cup. "I do have some work to do," she told him.

He stood up. "You're excused, Waring."

"Thanks for the coffee." She was self-conscious under his gaze, feeling it against her back as she walked away.

Chapter Ten

During her three-till-eleven in the evening shift, Stacy took advantage of her long mornings and days off to explore the island, finding a white strip of beach available to one and all not six blocks from the hospital. She went shopping once more to buy a one-piece bathing suit of soft yellow that clung to her slender figure in all the right places. Still rather thin, she looked healthier since she spent time lying in the sun and swimming in the surf, which made her use plenty of the right muscles. The low-blood problem she had encountered after losing the baby seemed determined to hang on, but she took her vitamins, pleased to feel her strength come back as good as ever. It was hard to imagine feeling anything but great in the sun that disappeared only for short periods, and the trade winds that blew warm every day.

Between her change of shifts she had four days off and hadn't yet made up her mind what to do with all that time off. She toyed with the idea of flying to Kauai, the Garden Isle, that the other nurses reported was even more beautiful than the island of Hawaii.

She had her doubts about that, but just might go. The flights weren't too expensive and she spent little money on anything else.

Better stop by to see Danny, she thought, *in case I do decide to go somewhere. I don't want him to think I've run away.* She smiled as she swung down the hall without changing from her uniform. Danny was the darling of the wing and basked in the love of everyone, but his favorite was Stacy.

He saw her coming down the hall and smiled, bright-eyed and chattering. As he grew tired she straightened his pillow, pulled the sheet up, and sat down to tell his favorite story of the Abomdable Snowman. His fingers played with hers as he smiled up at her and said, "Stace, it doesn't hurt anymore." His fingers grew still, and Stacy, startled, stared down at him as his eyes closed.

"Danny?" There was no response. "Danny!" Her hand hit the alert button, and she pumped the still chest. Nothing.

Instantly the room filled with people. Her shocked gaze locked with Dr. Grant's. "Get out, Waring," he ordered.

She didn't move. He grasped her shoulders and turned her to the door. She whirled. "No."

He took her arm, shoved her outside, and said, "Leave." The door swung shut.

She must have been walking the beach for hours, and didn't remember changing her uniform for a lemon-yellow T-shirt and beige shorts. She was barefoot. She stumbled toward the retaining wall, then sat down, drawing knees up under her chin. Her throat hurt all the way down into her chest. She watched, wide-eyed, as the tide came rushing in, the waves breaking forward and retreating, leaving the sand clean and white. A foam-crested wave coming toward her shimmered and broke apart as the tears spilled over, and she was sobbing, her head down on her knees, crying for all the times she couldn't in the past. The baby she had never been able to grieve over; the heart that shattered for lack of love; for all the unwanted love she carried in her heart for Greg; for all the Dannys who spread sunshine a short while and were gone. The harsh sobs tore through her chest, noisy and rasping. Her fist, crammed against her mouth, did nothing to stop the punishing gulps choking her.

She took the square of white placed in her hand without thought and tried to stop the tears.

"All right, Waring. That's enough."

Dr. Grant's face swam in front of her. "Go away," she told him.

"I want you to stop crying," he commanded in a voice that would stop the sun from shining if he so asked.

She pulled away from him. "I don't care what you want. Leave me alone." She dropped her head to her knees again as her sobs started anew, her slim body shaking with the uncontrollable force.

His hand lifted her chin, and as she turned her head away he slapped her, hard. Eyes blazing through tears spilling over, she went at him. Her arm swung in a short arc, the flat of her hand hit him across the mouth, and she was up and running before he realized what she was doing. Her strong tanned legs were no match for his long ones and he caught her, yanking her around to face his anger. She took a step backward and they went down in a tangle of arms and legs, Stacy hitting the sand first, his body knocking the wind from her. She lay still, tear-drenched eyes staring into his face.

"Are you all right?" he asked, his voice unexpectedly gentle.

"Yes." Her voice broke on the one word.

He pushed thick bangs away from her eyes, brushing sand from her cheek. She watched his mouth, a straight stern line, as it came closer to hers. She closed her eyes, feeling the firm coolness of his lips and the sand against the back of her head as the pressure on her lips increased. Her hands rested on his shoulders, and when he raised his head, she ran the tip of her tongue over the mouth he had just kissed, liking the masculine taste of it. It was somehow a comforting feeling as she remembered how long it had been since her last kiss.

"Did anyone ever tell you a kiss should be sweet, not salty?" he asked, smiling down at her.

She didn't answer, and he shifted his body, relieving the pressure from hers. Taking her hands from his shoulders, he pulled her to a sitting position. Her indrawn breath caught on a shuddering sob.

"Don't start that again, Waring," Dr. Grant's voice dared her.

She kept her head turned away from him. "What I don't need is the great Dr. Grant to lecture me. I was here first, so find you somewhere else to walk." She felt the tears starting again. "I'm not through crying and if you can't stand tears, the beach is certainly big enough for both of us."

Her body trembled and she dug her hands into the sand. He reached for her, pulling her into his arms, and she turned her face against the terry cloth of his shirt, letting the tears fall. He held her, his arms protective as her slender frame shook, giving way to all the hurt pent up too long. The sobs were no longer noisy, tears came steadily but quiet now, since she didn't fight to keep them back. When she could cry no more, she lay against him, her body jerking occasionally. He hadn't said another word.

Still without speaking, he lifted her to her feet, and, one arm around her, started walking. In a few moments he opened a car door.

"Did you have sandals?" he asked, getting in behind the wheel.

"I don't remember." Her voice was husky.

He pulled the car away and a little later he stopped. She looked up, saw they were in the driveway of a small bungalow, a yard rioting with hibiscus, ginger, and orangeberry bushes, the vibrant colors shining in the twilight.

"What a lovely place," she said.

Inside it was larger than it seemed from the outside. They entered a long wide room, spacious, with simple but elegant furniture in heavy rattan.

As if by magic, a man appeared, slim and dark skinned, smiling at them. "Colie, this is Stacy. Do you have any snacks we could eat?"

Colie bowed. "Yes, sir." He disappeared.

"The bath is that way. Perhaps you'd like a shower."

She stared at him. "This is your house, and you expect me to take a shower?"

"If you take a look at your face, and the sand in your hair, you might change your mind." He smiled. "And what's wrong with my house?"

She ignored the question. "You look human when you smile."

The green-flecked eyes narrowed as he opened his mouth, changed his mind, pointed down a short hall. "The bath is there. I'll get you something to put on."

The something he brought her was one of his own terry robes. She belted it around her, rolling the sleeves over and over to let her hands show through. It went almost to her bare feet. Her reflection in the mirror showed swollen eyes and a red nose. The short, dark hair curled in a damp fringe around her face.

Beautiful, she thought.

She walked with slow steps back to the room where she had left Dr. Grant. He was standing by a bar she hadn't noticed before. He looked at her and grinned, pulling a stool out for her.

"Good fit," he said as she perched on the stool near him. He studied her pale face, taking in the moist shadows remaining under her eyes.

The snacks turned out to be tiny sandwiches with a delicious filling she couldn't identify. She ate, not remembering the last meal she'd had, but shook her head when offered more.

Colie came, handing her a steaming mug of liquid

with a strange, pungent aroma, pineapple among other things.

"What is it?" she asked.

Dr. Grant answered her. "Colie's specialty. Drink up."

She tasted it and made a face. "It's strong."

"Drink it," he ordered.

She looked at him, ready to argue, but his serious expression stopped her. She drank.

He took the mug from her. "Let's sit over here where you can relax," he said, indicating the heavy rattan chair near the window as he sat on the couch facing her.

"How did you know I'd be at the beach?" she asked, eyeing him over the mug as he handed it back to her.

"Boyd told me it's your favorite hangout."

Anna didn't swim, so she seldom visited the beach that Stacy loved, but knew that was about the only place she went with any regularity.

A few more sips from the mug and she was glad she was in a chair. Her body relaxed; her eyes grew heavy. Realization came a little late. "There's something in that drink," she accused.

"You're right," he said, his voice muted through the effects of the drink.

That was all she remembered. She felt his arms lifting her, smelled a faint after-shave, then nothing.

SHE LAY still in the strange bedroom, remembering the previous day. A heavy sadness lingered for Danny, as she knew it would for a long time. The fact that she had known he couldn't live with the disease eating away at him didn't alter her feelings. *We can have our dreams, Danny, but miracles take longer.* Her tears had not all been for Danny; they had been for her dreams too.

She sat up, expecting her head to hurt from whatever drink she had, but she felt pretty good, considering. Her T-shirt and shorts lay folded neatly on a chair with thick-soled thongs nearby. And a toothbrush. Her eyebrows climbed. Some service.

She came out of the shower, dressed, and hesitated. The house was quiet, not a sound from anywhere. The bedroom where she had slept faced the street, and she stood looking at the bright sunlight on thick green lawns, palm trees framing the edge of it. Few cars moved, and she wondered what time it was. Her watch had stopped.

She made her bed and folded Dr. Grant's robe across the foot of it. Opening the door, she found herself in a wide hall with doors leading in several directions. She walked till she came to an open door and went through it, recognizing the room they had been in the night before. It was a wide room with an oval table spread with a snowy lace tablecloth and a huge bowl of fresh-cut flowers in the center. In the corner was the bar she remembered only vaguely sitting at with Dr. Grant before she unwisely drank something before inquiring what it was. She did ask, she recalled. He just neglected to tell me the entire truth. He was right as always, though, because it had helped her through some bad hours.

Dr. Grant was a very eligible bachelor, a fact she

heard often enough with all the swooning and sighs she was exposed to in the dormitory and on duty.

"He never has dated any nurses," one girl told Stacy when she first arrived, perhaps thinking to see her succumb to his charms as others before her had done.

"He doesn't have to," someone else added. "He has the pick of any elite crop he wants. why should he stoop to lowly nurses?"

"Because he can't do without us," the first voice said, amid general laughter.

Stacy's feelings for Dr. Grant weren't love oriented, but bordered on the verge of hero worship due to his ability as a doctor. She had been in the operating room with him enough to recognize genius when she saw it, even if no one had mentioned it to her. And where he wasted no compassion on the nurses, he had it to spare for his patients. She knew Danny had been a favorite of the famous doctor, as well as the nurses.

Stacy touched the fresh flowers, recognizing only ginger and the purple baby orchids in the bright plants. They were mostly of tropical origin, and she recognized few other than roses and jonquils. And barrel cactus.

Coming to the door opposite the one she had entered, she made a left turn through an archway that led into a terrazzo tiled area. To one side was a breakfast bar, two stools upholstered in coral print, and beyond that was Colie, busy at a gas range and oven installed in an island in the center of the kitchen.

His back was to her, and she hesitated, but he sensed her presence, turned, and grinned. "Breakfast in five minutes. Okay?"

He moved with practiced efficiency and placed a plate in front of her in less than the time he gave her. She ate as if it were going out of style. Pancakes and sausage, strawberries with whipped cream, and coffee, strong and hot.

Colie was of Oriental extraction, but there Stacy's identification of origins ended. She didn't pretend to know nationalities and frequently mixed them even in her thoughts. Devoted to Dr. Grant, it appeared, Colie certainly was a great cook, and his grin was contagious. He surveyed her now as she ate, nodding his head in appreciation of her appetite.

"You were crying last night. Is there something wrong that I can fix?" His question was gentle, not prying.

She was quiet a moment, green eyes hiding behind the heavy lashes, then replied, "Everyone needs a good cry now and then, Colie, and I guess it was my turn." The lashes swept upward, and she smiled. "It was kind of Dr. Grant to let me stay, and thank you for feeding me." She couldn't talk about Danny, not yet. It had taken him to set off tears for every hurt she felt.

"My pleasure." He stood up. "Would you like to see the gardens?"

He led her through the kitchen door onto a screened patio that opened into the garden, where orchids bloomed in profusion and hibiscus demanded growing room. The neatly rocked borders separated ginger from roses, and hollyhocks from palm trees. A redwood fence created privacy, and beyond that she heard the pounding surf.

"You're right on the beach," she said in surprise. "No wonder it didn't take long to get here."

"It's a block or so away," Colie told her. "But convenient."

They returned to the kitchen, Stacy's eyes busy absorbing the beauty of the yard. She felt a gentle ache as she looked at the blue sky drenched in early morning sunlight. Everyone who lived in Alaska should be allowed to visit Hawaii at least once, she thought.

As Colie reached to open the door Dr. Grant was there. He smiled, showing even, white teeth. "Better?"

I keep being surprised at how handsome he is, Stacy thought, taking in the blue polo shirt and denim shorts. "Aren't you working today?"

"I've been on my rounds and am off for the rest of the day." His expression was grave, and she knew without a doubt that he had been to see Danny's family. He went on, "My sister, Kay, and her husband have a ranch across the island near Kamuela, about fifty miles from here, and we have an invitation to ride out for the day. How about it?"

"A ranch?"

"Yes." He smiled at her. "Believe it or not, we have ranches here big enough to rival Texas."

"You mean cattle ranches?" Her expression was unbelieving.

"Lots of them." He stood up. "Shall we?"

In the carport he unlocked the door of his unpretentious white sedan, then closed it as she settled against the wine velour seat. He didn't talk as he guided them through the quiet streets to the highway

Miracles Take Longer 173

that ran along the shoreline for several miles before turning inland toward the mountains.

"We'll take the scenic route over the mountains. Takes a little longer to drive that way but it's well worth it," he said. "Have you been to the other side of the island?"

"Well, I doubt we saw all there is to see but I did take a tour when I first came here to all the tourist places. We went on the highway circling the island."

"This route takes you across the highest mountain peak on the island, Mauna Kea, then down past the Kohala Mountains that separate the shores of the island. Quite impressive." He looked at the girl beside him, her face half turned from him, thick long lashes reaching upward toward the straight winged brows as the wide green eyes took in the spectacular view that he knew mere words would never describe.

Stacy's mind was busy making comparisons to places she had been so recently, coming to the conclusion that it was impossible to have three states so different as Arizona, Alaska, and Hawaii, even with the indisputable evidence of having been in all three. She shook her head in wonder.

"How old are you, Waring?" Dr. Grant's abrupt question interrupted her musings.

"My first name is Stacy," she said. "I'm—I'll be twenty-eight tomorrow." She had forgotten the date was so near.

"We'll have to celebrate the occasion." He glanced at her, then back at the road. "You haven't lived long enough to know how hard some of life's punches are, Waring. They get harder and more frequent." After a moment, when she didn't answer, he went on. "Danny is just one of your harder punches."

No, she thought. *Don't hit me any harder and no more often than once in a lifetime.* She kept her face toward the car window, no longer seeing the lush landscape. *Let him think all the tears are for Danny. He doesn't need to know most of them are for me.*

He went on, "One of the first things you learned when you started nurse's training was not to get personally involved with your patients, right?" He knew she was much too fond of Danny for her own good but he had let her go, knowing Danny had little chance for survival, and he needed Stacy as much as she needed him.

She turned to look at him. "Yes," she said. "And the first thing impressed on me at Grant Memorial was no fraternizing with the untouchable Dr. Grant." She drew in a deep breath as she watched his profile. "If Maureen Bowden knew I'd spent the night in your house, she'd have me strung up by my toenails." She laughed, picturing the look on Anna's face too, if she ever found out about it.

Maureen Bowden was a stickler where the conduct of her nurses was concerned. She made it clear at all her bull sessions with them that no nurse-doctor relationship would interfere with their duties, that any dating would be discreet, and that no indiscretion would be tolerated. Stacy knew better than to think Dr. Grant would be intimidated by Mrs. Bowden, but he made his own rules about not dating nurses, and woe be unto Stacy if she did anything to start rumors flying around the hospital.

His kiss of the evening before had been nothing more than his effective way of stopping her tears—and even that had failed. There would be no love for Dr. Grant as other than a doctor until doomsday, when her love for Greg would surely die.

Even the thought of Greg could still stir her insides, crowding out any other emotions. She forced herself to breathe slowly and flexed her fingers out of the clenched fists in her lap.

As they turned from the highway onto a state-maintained road, Dr. Grant said, "Kay and Don's property starts about a mile from here and covers five thousand acres." A few minutes later they began seeing cattle in scattered small herds grazing over the dark green grass. The mountains seemed to frame the countryside into a tourist's dream of a postcard. She saw the structure of the low, rambling ranch house while they were some distance away set among palms and banana trees, huge coconuts nestled in clusters thirty feet up the palms that she had never seen grow that tall. Craning her neck in every direction, Stacy took in as much as she could before the car stopped in the long, circular driveway.

The family gathered around to greet them as Dr. Grant got out of the car and walked around to open Stacy's door. "Stacy, this is Kay and Don." He hugged the pretty woman, who was an older version of himself, including the green-flecked eyes. Don, slim and darkly tanned, greeted her with a friendly drawl that could have come from Texas.

Kay took her arm. "Stacy, these are our children, Bryan, Janette, and Heidi." Stacy smiled warmly at the children, remarking at their resemblance, and Heidi, blond pigtails swinging down her back, ran over and took Stacy's hand, a broad grin across her face.

Thus welcomed into the family like an old friend rather than a stranger, Stacy caught the enthusiasm of the three Reynolds children, and the afternoon passed in a pleasant haze of enjoyment, the tragedy of Danny pushed to the back of her mind for the moment.

As they prepared to go for a horseback ride across the open range, Stacy told Bryan, "It's been a long time since I rode a horse. Give me a gentle one." For a brief instant she thought of Waco, her sorrel pony on the Mati and her fateful ride on him her first visit to Greg's office, then shrugged the thoughts away, determined to enjoy being on the ranch.

Dr. Grant was right. It was a huge ranch and had it not been for the knowledge that she was on an island in the middle of the Pacific Ocean, she could have believed she was in Texas.

Dinner was a barbecue outside, corn on the cob, and enormous pans of fried potatoes. Stacy curled up on a glider, stuffed, watching Dr. Grant walk toward her.

She sat up. "Are you ready to leave?"

"I am," he said, "but why don't you stay and I'll be back tomorrow afternoon?"

Kay joined them. "Do stay, Stacy. We don't have many visitors and we're enjoying you so much." She looked up at her brother. "Mark doesn't come often enough." She hugged him and asked, "Can't you stay too?"

He shook his head. "I'll be back about four tomorrow."

"Great," Kay told him. "We'll be looking for you."

Stacy watched Dr. Grant's car pull away and turned back to Kay. "I feel like I could wake up any time and find it's all a dream." She shook her head and asked, "Have you ever been to Alaska, Kay?"

"No, Stacy, I'm afraid we're rather stay-at-homes."

Stacy grinned at her. "Doesn't matter. You wouldn't believe it, anyway. Or Arizona either." Her eyes followed deep green of the landscape to the green blue of the mountains, and from there toward the water she knew was just out of sight. "I had to see it before I believed it."

As the sun went down in flaming clouds behind Mauna Kea, Stacy yawned. "To bed, Stacy," Kay said. "You're exhausted." Stacy didn't protest and, in bed a few minutes later, was soon sound asleep. After all the fresh air, it was the best sleep she could remember, and she awoke early, showered and was wishing she had a clean change of clothes when there was a knock on the door. Kay called, "Stacy?"

She opened the door. "Good morning."

Kay smiled. "Bryan's shorts and shirt are as close as I could get to your size. Try them."

She pulled the denim shorts on, zipped them, turned them loose and they slid halfway down her slim hips.

Kay laughed. "My goodness, Stacy, we'll have to put some meat on you. Good thing those pants have a belt. Here. Put the shirt on, and let's see. Maybe we'll have to get a pair of Jan's shorts if this belt doesn't hold them."

The shorts stayed up with the help of the belt, and the red and white striped shirt was filled out in the right places, as Bryan hadn't been able to do. After breakfast the three children led her on a merry chase of swimming, horseback riding, and going over much of the ranch in Don's Jeep.

Sitting astride the small mare Bryan saddled for her, Stacy gazed over the dark green meadow they had crossed. A wide stream flowed from north to south out of the mountains in the distance, and the water sparkled like crystal. Across the stream and up the next hill were a hundred or more head of black cattle, which Bryan had named for her and she had already forgotten. All she knew was that it was an eye-resting, beautiful picture.

We need about half of this on the Mati and we could have all kinds of gardens and cattle instead of dried-up peas and corn, and scrawny ponies. All the world was a contrast, she thought, but no place came close to the Mati, and that could in no way be termed a compliment. As a matter of fact, the Mati had no plusses on its side. *Unless you count Rachel and Star, and they haven't a Chinaman's chance of changing much of the reservation's luck.* An Indian with a Chinaman's chance. She smiled at her comparison.

It was three thirty when Dr. Grant appeared. He looked tired, Stacy thought. *I wonder if he ever admits he's human enough to get tired and feel other emotions.* She found herself wondering for the first time what kind of women he dated.

He took in her outfit of Bryan's denim shorts and red striped shirt, grinned, and nodded. "Happy birthday," he said.

Her eyes widened in surprise; she had forgotten. As they finished dinner out on the huge enclosed patio, laughing and teasing like old friends, Kay excused herself and went inside the house.

Don rose and went with her, and when he came back, he was carrying a birthday cake in the shape of a nurse's cap, with twenty-eight candles.

"Oh" was all the expression Stacy could manage. Searching out Dr. Grant's smiling face, she said, "Colie?" He nodded.

There was a chorus of "Happy Birthday," then Heidi said, "Make a wish, Stacy, and blow out all the candles."

Closing her eyes for a second, she thought, *Someday—my very own miracle*. She drew a deep breath, let it go, and all the candles went out. For the first time in more than a year, she forgot Greg for more than an hour.

"You have tomorrow off?" Dr. Grant asked as they ate cake and ice cream.

"Yes. Then it's eleven-till-seven shift again."

"Let's stay here tonight, and I'll get you back to the dorm early."

Late that evening with everyone else in bed, Stacy wandered toward the corral in the moonlight. The smell of ginger teased her senses, bringing memories surging into her consciousness.

How long did you remember things that hurt so? Why couldn't you sift out the pain and remember only the good? Because a year of brutal memories smothered the few months of happiness, erasing all the sweetness.

"Can't you sleep, Waring?" It was Dr. Grant.

"I've rested so much since I've been on the ranch that I'm not sleepy."

They walked on in silence, until he asked, "Are you still crying over Danny?" He was looking at her face, silvery streaks shining on her cheek.

"No." She looked around at him. "It's hard to accept the fact that people like you can't help the Dannys of the world. How about you? Don't you feel frustrated and angry?" She hadn't even noticed the tears until he mentioned them.

He glanced at her. "Yes. All of that."

Surprised by his admission, she stopped. "How do you resolve it in your own mind, then?" she asked. "Do you cry inside?"

"You're being a smart aleck, Waring," he said.

"No," she denied, "I don't think so. I cry and you call me hysterical and a woman, but you, being the great Dr. Grant, can't afford to shed tears in public. Therefore, to keep your sanity, you cry inside." She paused, curiosity in her voice as she talked to Mark Grant, the man, not the doctor. "Or is that why you pick on your nurses, getting it out of your system?"

He stood looking down at her. "I wasn't aware I picked on nurses."

"Well, you do." She walked on. "Especially Anna. You scare her to death.

"But not you?"

She hesitated, then shrugged. "No, Dr. Grant, you

don't scare me. I love working with you, and I don't scare easily."

They had reached the corral and stopped to lean against it. "Where's your family, Waring?"

"I don't have any," she told him.

"None?" She could feel his curiosity.

Greg. A lost baby girl. Star and Rachel. No one. "I may have a husband somewhere," she said.

"What?"

"I was married for a while. We're separated."

He waited for her to go on, and when she remained silent, he asked, "What happened?"

She swallowed twice before she answered him. "He didn't love me."

"Did you love him?" Dr. Grant's voice seemed to come from far away.

Does the sun shine? Does the ocean have water? "Yes."

They were quiet. Night birds called across the fragrant breeze. She heard animal sounds from beyond the corral.

"How long have you been separated?" he asked after a long silence.

"A year."

"Did you file for divorce?"

"No. I told him to do as he pleased about a divorce or annulment."

"Annulment? If you lived together as man and wife, Waring, you can't get an annulment."

She thought about it, moved her slim shoulders, and said, "Some states allow annulment if you can prove desertion. I deserted."

"Haven't you ever checked to see if he got a divorce?"

"No."

"Waring," his voice was impatient. "You can't live forever not knowing if you're married or divorced."

"Why not?" She wanted to add another question, What difference does it make? but refrained, knowing he would have a comeback for that too.

"That's an unreasonable answer if you think about it," he said.

She thought about it and decided it was unreasonable, but she let it go. They turned back toward the house.

As they said good night, he reached and tumbled her hair. "You're a strange one, Waring."

Sleep was an illusion as she lay in bed, remembering other nights in Greg's arms.

Chapter Eleven

Mark's preoccupation was evident as he drove them toward Hilo, and Stacy was content to sit quietly beside him. He had accomplished what he set out to do. Kay, Don, and the three youngsters had taken her mind off Danny for a while, and even Greg had retreated into her subconsciousness for a few hours.

Dr. Grant's voice interrupted her thoughts. "You should get out more, Waring. You stay in that dormitory too much alone."

"I'm okay," she said.

"There are some nice young doctors around. Why don't you go out with them?"

"I'm married, remember? And I don't stay alone very much."

"You don't wear rings. Have you told anyone else you're married?"

"No."

"Has Gorman or Jared asked you out?" he persisted.

Grinning, she replied, "You know they have. But, then, they ask everyone out." Doctors Gorman and

Jared, the two youngest interns, enjoyed their status as resident playboys at Grant Memorial.

"Good-looking young guys."

She turned to look at him. "You aren't married, Dr. Grant. Why not?"

"Never thought it necessary," he said, grinning at her.

"Haven't you ever been in love?" she asked, curiosity in her voice.

"Lots of times."

"Nothing serious?"

"I fall seriously in love a couple of times a year. That way I keep in practice." He laughed. "My well-meaning friends tell me what I'm missing, but I doubt I'm missing much."

Lush green landscape glided by, and Stacy mused aloud, "You're wrong," she told him. "There are the sleepless nights when you toss and turn, your eyes burn, and your heart aches. The times when you reach out and there's no one there. You wonder, finally, what you did to deserve this, and you make up your mind to forget, but there's the old hostility between the mind and the heart, which allows them both to betray you." She turned to look at him. "So, you see, Dr. Grant, you are missing something." She went back to watching the scenery. "Take it from one who knows, go on missing it."

"You're beginning to sound like a martyr, Waring." His voice was sharp. "Don't go feeling sorry for yourself."

"You don't think I have a right to that?"

"No. You're young, healthy, your whole life ahead of you. Make use of it."

What about the life behind me? she wondered. *What do I do with that?*

Sudden resentment filled her. *What right has he to criticize me and tell me what to do?* Her voice was silky as she said, "Tell you what, Dr. Grant. I'll be glad to date you. Just a casual relationship that will get me out of the dorm and you won't have any worry about serious entanglements, a good setup for both of us."

His mouth was a straight line as he swung his head to look at her. "I make it a practice to never date my nurses, Waring."

She snapped her answer back at him. "Great. You don't dictate to me about going out and I promise not to ask you to go out with me."

It was a moment before he laughed softly, "Waring, you certainly know how to get your point across." He shook his head. "It's a deal."

AT WORK THERE was no change in their relationship. She asked no quarter, and was offered none. He was the same critical and demanding Dr. Grant as he had always been.

Without discussing or planning, Stacy was included in regular visits to the Reynoldses' ranch when she was off and fell into a habit of stopping at Dr. Grant's on her way to or from the beach. He was seldom home, and she helped Colie in the yard or the kitchen, listening to his tales of life on the islands. He fascinated her with his zest for life, and his devotion to Dr. Grant. His great love was cooking, and Stacy loved to try all the exotic dishes he made for Dr. Grant's entertaining.

She was perched on a stool in the kitchen late one afternoon when Dr. Grant walked in. He ran his hands through her short hair as he passed.

"If she gets in your way, Colie, throw her out." He opened the refrigerator to reach for a Coca-cola.

Colie grinned at him and winked at Stacy, "Stacy's good company."

"How's the dinner coming?"

Colie was enthusiastic, "Right on time."

Dr. Grant looked at Stacy as she sat with her tanned legs wrapped around the stool. "If you'll put on a dress, you can come to the dinner party."

"I don't have a dress, but thanks anyway." She shook her head. "Too high class for me, and too many beautiful ladies chasing you. I'd be green-eyed with jealousy."

His laugh rang out in the kitchen. "You're certainly green-eyed."

"Can I call you Mark?" she asked, looking up at him. "I promise not to get too familiar around the hospital."

His eyebrows went up. "What brings that about?"

She thought about it a moment before answering. "I don't know. You just seem more like a Mark than a Dr. Grant when I'm here."

"Tell me, Waring, if I said no, would you listen?"

"Yes, but I wouldn't like it."

His eyes went over the small figure with its serious expression. "Call me Mark. And go buy a dress to wear so you'll look like a girl."

"You mean I don't?"

"No. You look like someone's kid sister getting under everyone's feet."

A long time ago someone had told her: "I have to get you on your feet to get you out from under mine." Who did he have under his feet now? she wondered, and sent her mind in search of material less likely to drive her crazy.

She slipped from the stool and went to Mark, putting her arms around his waist. "You're rather sweet, Dr. Grant. If I weren't already madly in love with Colie, I'd fall for you." She turned away from his surprised look, helped herself to a handful of cookies from the plate, and said, "I gotta go before your guests arrive. Thanks, Colie." And with a wave she ran down the path and up the street, across the small park, toward the dormitory.

Mark Grant's eyes followed the slim figure as it disappeared from his sight. Since the day she had challenged him to date her if he was so interested in her going out, neither of them had mentioned it, and he was well aware that she worked, swam, and visited Colie, and nothing more. He could almost hate the man who had married her and left her, but he didn't know enough of the circumstances, and he was almost certain he'd never learn from Stacy.

In Saturday's paper Stacy read with interest the account of the elegant party at Dr. Mark Grant's home. There was a picture of Mark with a lovely girl named Sybil Courtney.

"You'd better be nice to him," Stacy said aloud to no one in particular. "Else you'll have me to answer to." She grinned. Probably scare the girl to death.

After gathering up her bathing suit and a towel, she headed for the beach and, after an hour of swimming, made her way to Mark's back door.

Colie greeted her. "Just the one I wanted to see. If I hold this ladder, could you climb up and put your hand through the opening there, and pull the vine through? My hands are too big."

"Sure." She got the vine and helped him thread it through the lattice work. "All your problems should be that small, Colie," she told him. She stood for a moment looking at the sprays of baby vanda orchids and strong straight shoots of birds of paradise, shaking her head. You had to see the colors to believe them, she decided.

He grinned his thanks. "Hungry?"

"I was hoping you'd ask," she said, climbing on her favorite stool. "Where's Mark?"

Colie placed a slice of watermelon on the table beside the thick pork sandwich. "He went to the airport to pick up someone coming about the hospital plans."

"Oh, that's right. He's gonna redo the dormitories. That's great." She concentrated on her lunch, doing justice to the melon and sandwich, sighing as she finished eating.

Turning, Colie watched her as she sat, chin in hands, staring at nothing, the green eyes narrowed against the brightness. In the one-piece yellow bathing suit and barefoot, she looked every bit of sixteen. Around her neck was a thin gold chain, the only jewelry he had ever seen her wear.

"I'd better run before your visitor arrives, Colie.

Wouldn't want him to think you're taking in beachcombers." She stretched. "Thanks for lunch."

She sauntered out the back door, alongside the flower beds, bending to pick a dark yellow and brown pansy, and around the carport. Mark was just getting out of the car with his guest, and she would have turned and run, but Mark had seen her.

"Good afternoon, Waring." His amused glance took in her outfit.

She stopped beside him, grinning. "Sorry, Mark. I was trying to get away before you got home."

She looked at the man standing quietly by, her eyes meeting the dark blue ones, narrowed in shock. Stunned, she stared at Greg, saw the disbelief in his face, the world turned upside down as pain knifed through her chest. For the second time in her life she fainted.

From darkness she fought her way up, opening her eyes to see Mark's concerned face. "What are you doing to me, Waring?" His voice was rough.

"Mark?" Seconds passed before she remembered what had happened. Turning her head, she saw Greg at the foot of the bed, his expression carefully guarded. *This can't be real,* she thought, closing her eyes again.

"Are we still married?" she asked, eyes wide now and full of questions.

His face didn't change. "Yes."

Her gaze came back to Mark, who stared first at her, then at Greg. "Greg is the husband I said I might still have."

Disbelief and confusion shook Mark's voice. "Your name is Fields?"

"Waring is my maiden name." She drew a shaky breath, looking back at Greg. "Why?"

"I'll never give you up, Stacy," Greg said.

"Never, Greg?" The bitterness in her voice surprised her. "It seems to me you gave up long ago. You were waiting for me to come back, maybe?"

"I looked everywhere for you, except Alaska. You hated cold weather so much, it never occurred to me you'd go there. After we heard a few words of a broadcast about the floods, we looked there too, but not the right place." She had forgotten the low vibrance of his voice, and its effect on her. "When the check came, I telephoned Anchorage, but you had already gone, and no one knew where."

Aware of Mark's hand holding hers tightly, she turned to look at him, her eyes dark and unreadable. She swung her feet from the bed, and Mark pulled her to a sitting position.

"Are you all right?" he asked.

"Yes. I have to go."

He stood up with her. "Maybe you'd better take one of Colie's drinks along."

"No, thanks, I'll be all right." She gave him a brief smile and, without a backward glance, ran out the front door and up the street, taking her familiar shortcut across the small park.

Why, out of all the architects Mark had presented his plan to, did it have to be Greg he elected? Why hadn't she thought about it herself? The day she and Mark had discussed the dormitories in the coffee shop at the hospital she should have had some kind of inkling of what was going on. Scrambled thoughts kept pace with her fast-moving feet, and stuck in her throat like so much Arizona desert sand was the knowledge that fifteen months of painful memories had left her unprepared for this. *It's just like it was yesterday,* she thought, resentment filling her. *All the fighting with myself for a year, wasted effort. Just seeing him again turns me inside out.* A harsh, dry sob all but strangled her.

The pain accompanied her as she went about the familiar duties, glad her reflexes remembered what she was supposed to do, whether she did or not. By three in the morning she was exhausted to the point that she began doing everything wrong.

When old Mr. Randall asked for a glass of warm milk to help him sleep, she took it to him and felt unfamiliar anger touch her when she found him asleep. She shook him none to gently and urged him to drink the milk. He mumbled and refused to open his eyes.

"Mr. Randall, since you asked for this special and I went out of my way to bring it, the least you can do is drink it. I have more patients than you to care for."

As she finished speaking, watery dark eyes looked up at her. "My name is Molina, Nurse."

Stacy gulped, seeing the man for the first time, and apologized profusely, then took the milk across the hallway to Mr. Randall.

Making her way into a bathroom with two bedpans, she let the door go, bumping one arm, spilling the contents down her front, and not only had to change her uniform, had to have a complete bath.

At six she started checking temperatures, having to

wake some of her patients who were inclined to be grumpy. Stacy felt grumpy too and wished for the end of her shift, one more hour, if she could make it.

She replaced the container of thermometers in the sterilizer, removing the next batch she would need, and dropped them, breaking three. She stood looking down at the mess, tempted to let loose with a scream. Only her stern self-discipline as a nurse saved her patients from a very rude awakening. She hadn't broken a thermometer since her first day in training.

At six thirty, groggy from lack of sleep and the horrible Saturday night duty, she got ready to leave her shift with Anna relieving her.

"Stacy, you know they're gonna renovate the dorms?" Excitement colored her voice.

"Yes, I heard," she said. "Think it will be an improvement?"

"The architect's from Arizona; supposed to be great." She sighed. "And is he ever handsome! You should see him."

"How long will he be here?"

"I heard all week. Just think, Stacy. While you're sleeping, he'll be walking around you. You know, if I were you, I'd stay awake all day."

As she got her coffee from the cafeteria line, Stacy thought, *I'll be awake, Anna. For what purpose, I don't know.* In the middle of the morning crowd of shift changers and visitors, Stacy sat, sipping the bitter coffee, miles away from it all.

I need Colie's drink, she thought. *I'll never make my next shift if I don't sleep. Tonight was a catastrophe—*

what will tomorrow night be if I don't get some rest? Her body felt tight and achy, her mind thick as if she were on heavy drugs.

She raised her eyes from the coffee as someone sat across from her, looking straight into the navy blue ones she loved so much. Greg's face was thinner than she remembered, and she looked with interest at the gray in his hair, not there when she had last seen him.

"Mark told me you'd be here," he said. "He knows you pretty well."

"Yes, I guess he does," she acknowledged, wondering at her ability to sit there, talking in a normal voice, every nerve in her body aware of Greg across from her. She braced her feet beneath the table.

"Are you living with him?"

I wish I were, Stacy wanted to tell him. I wish I had a different man every night, then I'd never think of you. But she replied as though he had remarked about the weather, "Mark doesn't fool around with married women."

Greg listened to the quiet reply to his insulting question, eyeing the suntanned girl across from him, jade-green eyes free of any expression, the way he remembered her. No love, no hate, empty. He wanted to apologize, but anything he would say now would make it worse. After a moment, when he knew she wasn't going to elaborate on her answer, he asked, "Do you have trouble sleeping during the day?"

She shook her head. "I usually swim awhile, and it's easy to fall asleep."

"Where do you swim?"

"Near the pier, not far from Mark's house." Her eyes dared him to comment. She stood up. "I'll see you."

"I'll be leaving the hospital about three thirty. Can we meet and talk?" He stood too, looking down at her, realizing how small she was.

Wondering what subject they would tackle, Stacy stared at him. "All right. I'll meet you on the beach by the pier at four." At his questioning look she said with a wry smile, "There isn't much privacy in the dormitories. Perhaps your plans will change that."

It was almost one when she got to Mark's place, and found the house empty. Colie was shopping for specialties to delight Mark's visitor from the mainland, no doubt. She wasn't hungry, and wandered through the living room, spotting an odd book on the coffee table. As she bent closer, her breath caught as she recognized the picture on the cover and read the title: *Miracle of the Desert* by Greg Fields. He had been working on a book when she left, but it had not been titled because he was still doing research. The cover was a picture of "The Place" just as she remembered it, just the way she had wanted the picture Star was painting to look. There were two views of the house: one from the front, showing the old mission-type architecture, with fortresslike columns. The second one showed the desert landscaping across the wide yard, facing the small mountain that was their bedroom—not theirs anymore. Greg's alone—or maybe he had someone else to share it now.

Picking the book up, she opened it to the fly leaf,

reading the inscription in gold print: TO STACY WITH LOVE—MIRACLES TAKE LONGER.

I know, Greg, she thought. *Some of them take forever.* She held the book in her hand, seeing the beautiful details of the house she loved. Because Greg planned and built it? Because that was where he had loved her? No, not loved her. Made love to her. There was a vast difference.

Placing the book back in the exact spot she had found it, Stacy went on into the spare bedroom. Stretching out across the width of the bed, she was instantly asleep.

Going to get his bathing suit, Greg passed the open bedroom door where Stacy lay, one hand curled against cheek, dark lashes wet and stuck together from the tears that never had a chance to fall. He had never seen her cry, not over the baby, not when he accused her of every wrong in the book. She had once threatened to stamp her feet and scream over the misery of the Indians, and he had seen the green eyes sparkle with anger more than once. But the tears, like stars on the black lashes, were the first he had seen.

The year she had been gone had changed her. She no longer looked fourteen; twenty-one maybe. Dark circles under her eyes were more pronounced because of her weight loss, her skin tight across the high cheekbones. The pale yellow bathing suit emphasized her smallness, but the rounded breasts still jutted firmly against the clinging material.

How many times in the past year he had tried to convince himself he would never see her again, that he had rid himself of her forever. Stacy, the loner, who had depended on herself all her life, made no demands on him, and who would never remain where she was unwanted. Rachel had told him, "You let her know she wasn't wanted." Only he knew he wanted her more than anything in the world.

As he stood looking down at her, she stirred, opened her eyes, and smiled up at him. "Sorry, I didn't get far. The bed looked so good, I couldn't resist."

His hands smoothed the short hair back from her face. "I'm glad you didn't change the color of your eyes, Stacy."

Leaning, he kissed her lips still curved from sleep, and her arms went around his neck, pulling him down to her. His hands, caressing the slim body, grew demanding in their quest for complete possession. She yielded, her body moving beneath him, lips parting with the bruising force of his kiss, sparking the painfully sweet response he always got from her.

The year's absence disappeared, and Stacy's whole being reacted to Greg's touch the way explosive chemicals reacted to each other. She heard his words murmured against her lips, her bare flesh responding to his exploring fingers, lifting her body upward to meet the hardness of his. Her hands, hungry for the touch of him, thrusting beneath his shirt, digging into his narrow waist, drew him closer.

His lips left hers, moving down her throat, skimming her cool skin till he found the soft swell of her breast. Stacy was wide awake now as the molten quicksilver filled her body and she looked at the silver-sprinkled dark head against her breast. As clearly as if he had spoken aloud, she heard again his words, "There was no love in our bargain."

"Let me go." She slid away from his surprised release of her, and stood up, moving away from him to the door, not looking at him as she waited for him to get his bathing suit, and led him toward the beach without another word.

Not speaking at all, they walked until they came to a turn in the shoreline and an area protected from the few people who used the beach. She spread the big towel she carried, and they sat watching the waves as she did so often.

Feeling again the terrible loss he experienced when she left him, Greg broke the silence. "I should have remembered how good you are at disappearing, Stacy. I had two private detectives looking for you, but they could never find any trace. Even after hearing about the floods, and Stubbs catching part of the broadcast, they didn't have any luck at all. Looking for a girl with thick braided hair didn't help them much."

"I know" was all she said.

"When the check came, I called the bank, and they referred me to Skowron Hospital. I talked to June Whiting, but she said you hadn't decided where you were going when she saw you last, and she had heard nothing from you." He watched her, but she didn't speak, and he went on after a moment. "Star and Rachel brought me the package you sent them, and the clipping about the floods and radio interview." He looked at Stacy, sitting so quietly near him. "I checked with the burn schools in San Antonio, Houston, and Atlanta, thinking you might go ahead with your schooling. Why, Stacy? Why didn't you write, at least to let me know you were all right?"

She took a long time to answer, remembering the long letter she had written to him, then torn to shreds. "I didn't have anything to say. You said everything for both of us."

"What do you mean?"

"Remember the last thing you said to me when you left for Denver? If you don't, I can quote it for you word for word."

"That I'd meet you at Dr. Parks's that Friday?"

"You wanted to see how soon we could have a baby." A feeling of utter hopelessness filled her as she waited for him to speak.

"Yes. And?" *My God, he doesn't even know what he did to me,* she thought. *Or doesn't care.*

A curious smile touched her mouth as she turned to look at him. "Without love, Greg. You said love wasn't in our bargain, and you were right. It wasn't, as I recall. You were very generous on your part, but I forgot about our bargain when I started to repay the loan, and did the unforgivable." She looked away from him, across the blue-green expanse of water that reflected its color in her eyes. "I fell in love. I should have been listening all the times you told me how naive I was, but it didn't register because I was so wrapped up in my little dream world. It was too late when I realized I wasn't naive, but stupid."

He started to speak, but she went on. "I don't know why I forgot the lessons I learned early in my life. By the time I was six, I knew not to expect too much of anyone or anything. By ten, I knew to expect very little. When I was thirteen, I expected nothing of anyone." She smiled at him. "How soon we forget."

"Stacy, don't." Greg's voice was low. "Do you mean what you said?"

"What?"

"You love me?"

"I'm getting over it." *In addition to having a conniving little mind, I also lie,* she thought, turning away.

"With Mark's help?"

Her eyes went back to him. "Yes, Mark helps. Not the way you mean, but he helps."

"For the record, there's been no one since you." His voice left no doubt what he meant.

When she remained silent, he said, "Star and Rachel have a little girl."

She sucked in her breath, and her eyes widened, looking alive for the first time. "When?"

"She's three months old. Her name is Stacy Lee." His voice held a smile.

Stacy was ashamed of the flame of jealousy she felt toward Rachel, as memories crowded in. Memories she seldom allowed to surface. The nursery, the mural, the painting. "Are they all right?"

"Yes. I see them on a regular basis. Star built them a nice, adobe house. He's worked with the VISTA representative and they've improved a lot of the conditions you were fighting at the Mati."

"I'm glad." She turned back to staring at the ocean and asked, "Did Star finish the painting for your birthday?"

"Didn't you see it finished?" His voice sounded odd, but she didn't look at him. She shook her head.

"You'll love it. It's on the cover of the book I brought Mark."

"Yes. I saw the book."

He caught her arm, turned her toward him. "Why didn't you tell me what the money was for? Why? It would have saved so much heartache."

"No, Greg. It would have saved heartache if you had loved and trusted me. Love and trust—you had neither. But then, I understood after you reminded me of our bargain, and I accept the blame for what happened. It's better to find out there's no love before there are children, and I'm glad you let me know."

His hands tightened. "As soon as I said that, I knew I was wrong, Stacy. I was hurt over losing the baby, and you didn't seem to care." She stared at him in disbelief. "Yes, I know," he went on. "Dr. Parks told me it had hurt you more than we could tell, but it would show in a different way once you let your guard down. Something you never did, Stacy. He was waiting to see how you responded during your six-week checkup. After I called from Denver, and you said two words, I wanted to call you again to tell you I was sorry for what I'd said. I decided to wait till morning, but you never answered the phone."

She shrugged away from him, and he dropped his hands. "I unplugged the phone and left early that morning." She felt nothing at what he was saying. None of it registered.

"I caught an earlier plane Thursday night. When I found your note with your ring, I thought you had run to Star and Rachel, so I went there, only to find they had a note from you too." He took a deep breath.

"I've never been so scared as when I realized they didn't know where you were. I haven't stopped looking for you since then. Come home, Stacy."

The green eyes flickered and looked away from him. "Why?"

"I love you. I want you back." He hesitated. "You do still have feelings for me, don't you?"

Her gaze came back to him. The blue, blue eyes; the lips that were so firm and felt so right on hers; the chin with only the suggestion of a dimple. No man had ever been loved as she had loved him, and yet...

"When did you start to love me?" Her breath was shallow and she didn't recognize her own voice.

He smiled. "The minute you walked into my office, plunked your little bottom down, and demanded that I do something for your people."

"I find that hard to believe, considering everything."

He sobered. "It took me longer than most people to see what was happening." He lifted a handful of sand, letting it sift through his fingers. "I realize your being pregnant was the best excuse I could offer for our marriage and not admit I was in love with you."

"But after living with me, then marrying me, you still thought I could have an abortion and get rid of our baby? You thought my conniving little mind was capable of planning it all?" Her voice thickened with anger. "That's not my idea of love. I don't need your guilt, Greg. I have enough of my own to deal with." She stood up, her eyes on him an instant longer. "No, Greg." And she was gone, running barefoot on the sand away from him.

"Stacy, wait."

She didn't hear him. She heard the roaring surf, saw the sea gulls dipping to the water, felt the warm sun on her body and the familiar iciness inside. After a year she was still running. She didn't stop till she reached her room.

Chapter Twelve

Mark called her into his office as she reported for duty Monday night. His later rounds completed, he was waiting for her.

Without preamble, he began. "I think you should sit down and talk to Greg. You owe him that much."

"I paid Greg all the money I owed him, and he got what he bargained for in the beginning. I can't give him back the several months of his life where I intruded. Besides, it's none of your business, Mark."

He studied the small tanned face, the unbelievable green eyes, the soft mouth that looked so vulnerable. He ignored her last statement.

"We were up most of the night while he told me the story, and I believe him when he says he loves you." He watched her small chin go up. "You never told me anything, Stacy. Would you like to tell me your side of it?"

"There aren't any sides, Mark. I'm sure Greg told you the truth. He might believe I lie, but he's always stayed close to the truth, as far as I know." Leaning against the corner of his desk, she let her finger make circles on the polished surface. "You've heard of a bad bargain, I'm sure. Well, that's what I made—a bad bargain. A mistake, if you will." She lifted her head and gave him a brief smile. "I must have been very young and naive, the way Greg told me I was."

Straightening her shoulders, she went on. "No, that wasn't it. I was just brought up in a totally different environment. We could have lived on two separate planets, so different we were. Are. We haven't changed noticeably."

Mark's eyes never left hers. "What caused the miscarriage?"

She winced, and a small sound escaped her lips. "You know how it is, Doctor. You've said it often enough. Nature's way of getting rid of the imperfects."

"Why didn't you or Dr. Parks explain that to Greg right then? Just because he's a world-famous architect, doesn't mean he has to understand everything," Mark explained reasonably.

Stacy stood there, watching Mark's face, finding it hard to realize he was defending Greg and blaming her. "Greg had already made up his mind I was trying to trap him and wasn't interested in any kind of explanation. He knew, to his own satisfaction, that it was an abortion, not a miscarriage, and nothing I could say would convince him differently."

Mark stared in shocked surprise. "Why, in the name of all that's holy, didn't you tell him what the money was for? Was it so hard for you to imagine how he might feel?"

"Yes." She placed her hands flat on the desk in

front of him. "Would you ever have accused me of such a thing?"

"I'm a doctor, Waring. As a good nurse, I'd expect you to know better. Greg was hurt and not thinking."

Her eyebrows made twin peaks. "Greg was hurt? Waring wasn't supposed to hurt, right?" She turned away from him. "You men are all alike. Don't hurt me, but don't feel bad if I break your heart; I really didn't mean to."

"Waring," he began, but she cut him short.

"Greg was always good to me, Mark. And gentle. He was the first, and only, man I belonged to; my first lover, my first husband. And the first to break my heart. Doesn't that sound old-fashioned?" She shook her head. "It wasn't his fault he couldn't love me, but I let myself forget one solid fact: I was repaying a loan from a businessman. And you know what happens when you forget about loans. The interest gets to be more than most people can afford, and I'm no exception. I just thought I was." She tried to stop the trembling inside her. "I've hurt like hell for over a year, and you expect me to forgive and forget, just like that? Uh-uh, Mark. Not yet. It's still raw inside."

"Do you still love him?"

It was her turn to stare at Mark, considering the question that sounded ridiculous to her since she could no longer remember when she didn't love Greg. "I don't really see that it makes any difference at all." Her shoulders drooped. "I'm on duty, Mark. I have to go."

"Just a minute, Waring." He eyed her, daring her to walk away. "Greg carries the clipping about your rescue mission, the radio interview, everything he could find. He had private detectives looking for you with a description that didn't come close, except for those green eyes. And do you know what kind of picture they had?"

She shook her head, knowing Greg had never taken pictures of her.

"He had one of you made with the sixth graders at the reservation when you were with VISTA. With the braids, and in that group, you looked like a twelve-year-old Indian. Your own mother would never have recognized you from that."

She smiled. "You're right. Mark. My mother wouldn't recognize me, nor would she care. She never did." She shrugged away her bitter thoughts. "I really do understand everything, Mark, very clearly. I should be a better loser than I am, that's all, but . . ." Her voice trailed off.

"You're not listening, Waring," he said. "Greg wants you back."

"For what? To have a baby for him without love? Did he tell you that too, Mark?" Anger shook her. "Of course, you don't need love to conceive a child; we all know you only need emotion." Her voice broke. "Anyone can do that, Mark."

"Is that what he said?"

She nodded. "We're even. He doesn't want love, but I caught a glimpse of what I thought it should be, and if I can't have love, then I don't want anything." She opened the door. "I really have to go." Turning, she looked back at him. "One other thing. He asked if you and I were living together." She grinned. "I should have said yes and shocked the pants off the untouchable Dr. Grant." She laughed out loud. "I really missed a golden opportunity." The door closed on Mark's incredulous expression.

The hours dragged as Stacy pushed herself to make the rounds usually so easy for her. Every step was made with the thought that she would never make it through the night. Off duty, she skipped her usual swim and visit with Colie, going straight to bed, sleeping till almost six o'clock.

She lay staring at the ceiling, wondering if she could get away with staying in bed forever. *I hurt somewhere,* she thought. *Pieces of my broken heart jabbing me, no doubt.* Her mind wandered on down the fuzzy path. *The ceiling needs painting. Maybe Greg will put in beams and indirect lighting.* She moaned. *How will I ever live through this week?*

It wasn't hard for her to avoid Greg. He had work to do and she stayed in her room except when she was on duty. Late Wednesday she ran into Mark making his rounds. "Do you think Kay and Don could put up with me a couple of days?"

"Running away again, Waring?" he asked.

"It's a nice place to run," she retorted.

"Greg and I will be out there Saturday and Sunday afternoon till he leaves. Will that bother you?"

She shook her head. "I'll come back to town Saturday morning. Will you let Colie take me out?"

"You'll be off by seven, won't you?"

"Yes."

Maybe it was just the graveyard shift, Mark thought, taking in the blue shadows under her eyes and obvious loss of weight. "I'll take you, Waring. I want to see Don about using some of his horses next month."

Dressed in jeans and a white T-shirt that hugged her slender body, showing off the small rounded breasts, Stacy felt as though she were moving in slow motion. A light tint on her lips and high cheekbones helped offset the circles under her eyes, but fatigue slowed her steps as she made her way to the cafeteria to wait for Mark.

I'm not going to be very good company, she thought. *I believe I could sleep forever.* Somehow, it was no surprise to see Greg sit down across from her. She regarded him, smiling a little, then said, "We're going to have to stop meeting like this."

"Mark had an emergency and asked me to drive you out to the ranch."

She shrugged as she rose from the chair. *Mark's still trying to patch us up, bless his heart. Why doesn't he just give up? I have.* The desolate feeling wasn't something new for her, but she had been beginning to think it wasn't as bad, until Greg came. Greg had an uncanny way of messing up all her well-laid plans.

In the car she asked, "You haven't been over the mountain yet, have you?" As he shook his head she instructed, "Once you get on the highway, it's a straight shot. The scenery is spectacular and it's a shame you're driving and can't look at it all. About forty miles from here, you'll see the sign for the Reynoldses'. If I'm asleep, call me."

He gave her a quick look, but she had already fastened the safety belt, and her head was back against the seat. His eyes took in the small face, framed by the short dark hair, the soft mouth he could almost feel touching his. "Tired?"

She didn't stir as she answered, "Incredibly."

He could never remember hearing Stacy complain of being tired. She never complained about anything, come to think about it. An unplanned pregnancy she accepted and set about doing what she thought should be done. His accusations—he didn't want to think about them.

"Did you know Mark and I are invited out to the ranch for the weekend?"

"Yes. I'll go back to town Saturday morning. No problem."

In the silence that followed she thought, *What would he say if I told him to stop and make love to me? Is it a sin to want your own husband? I must be going crazy,* she decided, and closed her eyes to doze. She no longer recalled what was right or wrong where Greg was concerned. Her one feeling was of lost opportunity to keep the man she believed would be the only one she'd ever love. It didn't matter what his accusations were, nor that he was determined she have a child for him without love. In her wildest fantasies he loved her, and that was all she had for the present, and it had taken her through the roughest times when otherwise she might not have survived. Even knowing they were dreams and would never be realized had been enough to give her the boost she had to have to keep going. Her body was intensely aware of Greg's physical presence, tingling with memories he must have long since forgotten. The kiss as she lay half asleep on Mark's bed sparked a response bringing home to her the realization that she had not forgotten Greg. On the contrary, her heart had returned to his keeping without regard for her wishes and in spite of her fight to control it.

From the day I met him, I never had a chance, she conceded.

With a conscious effort she sat up, saying, "That's Mauna Kea over to our right. The Reynolds children will be delighted to show you around. I think they know every inch of this island."

Greg wasn't looking at the scenery, but at Stacy. Her eyes looked swollen and she kept blinking in an effort to keep them open.

"The turn is over this ridge, and you're on the ranch."

Mark had evidently alerted the family they were coming, because Heidi was waiting for them. She hugged Stacy. "Can you stay all weekend?"

"Well, most of it, Heidi. This is Greg Fields, a friend of Mark's." She looked at Greg. "Heidi is one of three beautiful Reynolds children." Her hand moved over the braids of dark blond hair.

Kay came to meet them, her hands outstretched. Greg had been invited to the ranch, but they had never met, and talked pleasantries for a moment, until Greg said, "I'd better get to work. Thanks for the invitation, Kay. See you later."

Kay slipped her arm through Stacy's as they turned toward the house. "How about breakfast, Stacy?"

"Would you mind if I grab a nap, Kay? I'm really bushed."

"Of course not. Come on."

Stretching out on the bed, she told Kay, "Don't let me sleep over a couple of hours." She sighed, feeling the firm mattress against her tired body.

It was noon when Kay went to call her. She was crumpled against the pillow, her cheeks unnaturally pink, her lips parted and dry, her breathing too heavy to be natural. She seemed so small, her body curled as though she were cold, looking not much bigger than one of Heidi's dolls.

"Stacy," she called. Stacy's eyes opened, but looked through Kay without seeing. The lids dropped, and she muttered unintelligible sounds, turning on her back, frowning as if in pain, and her hand rubbed at her side.

Kay touched her face. It was hot. She didn't hesitate, and her call to Mark was paged over the hospital system. A moment later he was on the phone.

"I hate to bother you, Mark, but Stacy's awfully warm, and I can't get any sense out of her."

"What happened?" he asked, his voice sharp, remembering the way she looked as she had talked to him the night before.

"Nothing since she's been here," Kay told him.

"Take her temperature. Leave the thermometer under her arm for five minutes, and call me back."

Real alarm was in Kay's voice when she called him a few minutes later. "Mark, it's a hundred and three degrees."

His indrawn breath did nothing to allay her fears. "Keep her covered. I'll be there as soon as I can."

It was an anxious hour before his car swerved into

the drive, and the thought occurred to Kay that he had broken a few speed limits over the mountain. She watched as Mark examined Stacy.

Her pulse was slow and light, her breathing shallow. "Stacy." He pushed her eyelids up, but the green eye was filmed, and she made no response.

He shook his head. "Did she say anything before she lay down?"

"No. Only that she was tired." Kay stared, frightened at Stacy's stillness.

Mark called the hospital. "Have Room One Hundred set up for complete blood and X-rays," he told Maureen. "I'm bringing Waring in." He answered her questions briefly.

Wrapping Stacy in the blanket Kay got for him, he lifted her easily and laid her on the backseat of his car.

"I'll call as soon as I can." He kissed Kay and said "Don't worry, Heidi" to the little girl staring in bewilderment.

A while later Stacy opened her eyes, seeing antiseptic white walls and tubes that looked as though they were attached to her. She tried to pull her arm away.

"No, Waring. Keep your hands off."

She saw two of Mark and blinked to clear her vision. Darkness closed in and, sighing, she went back to sleep.

In the distance she heard voices. She struggled to get her eyes open, but the lids were weighted. One voice sounded like Greg's, but she knew it was part of her imagination. Arizona was far, far away.

"Greg?" Uncertainty clouded her question, but she needed verification that he wasn't really there.

"Yes, I'm here."

Well, you're not supposed to be, she thought. *I left you on the mainland twice, so...* "Why?"

"Stacy." His voice was a whisper that faded from her hearing.

"I hurt," she complained.

"I know, honey." That sounded like Mark. Honey? Mark calling her honey. She smiled, wincing as she felt the sting of a needle, and oblivion.

Reality worked its way into her consciousness in bits and pieces. The glucose bottle above her swung gently through the fog of pain and drugs, like some monstrous apparition from her nightmarish dreams. Where did all the white come from? Alaska. The snow, the glare from the long, long days, all ran together with her double shifts. *I'm tired. June will have to get someone else to work.* She floated. *I'm not in Anchorage. I work for Mark.*

"Waring?" He was there as if dreamed up by her thoughts.

Mark stood over her, his face worried, tired lines around his mouth, shadows under his eyes. "Hi," she said. Her face felt tight as she tried to smile at him.

"Hi? Is that all you can say after all this time?" Gentle hands touched her throat, her side.

"How long?"

"Today is Monday." He sat on the side of the bed.

Frowning, she tried to fit the pieces together, not too successfully. "I'm too tired." Even to her own ears, her voice sounded like a fretful child.

"Stacy, have you had any trouble like this before now?" Mark's voice was no nonsense, and if he called her Stacy, he must mean business. She could count on one finger the times he had called her by her first name.

"No. I've always been healthy."

"How about after your miscarriage?" he insisted.

"Well." She hesitated. She was in for a scolding from Mark when he found out she was late for her checkup. "My red blood count was low, and I had a little infection."

"Little infection? What kind?" Trust Mark to want specifics.

"Blood and kidney."

"What treatment?"

"Antibiotics."

"For how long?"

"Six months."

His hands stopped their movements over her body. "Six months? A little infection, Waring?" He glared at her. "I think you'd better tell me the whole story. Don't leave anything out."

She sighed. "I had some trouble with hemorrhaging, and I'm still on medication." She named the drug.

"Yes, Kay found that in your handbag." Mark picked up her hand that moved restlessly on the sheet. "Did your doctor give any indication if he thought you'd have trouble carrying another child?"

She shook her head, beginning to have trouble keeping her eyes open. "He said I should be all right. Mark, don't fuss." Her mind drifted into a drugged emptiness, her hand relaxing in his.

The room was almost dark when she opened her

eyes again, and she struggled to clear up what was a dream and what had happened. Her mind was slow in accepting any of the facts she tried to sort out, or any of the things she remembered. She saw Greg as he looked when she walked around the carport at Mark's house when he first arrived; saw him as they talked on the beach when he told her he loved her and wanted her back; and found herself wondering why he felt obligated to say things not required of him. Guilt. She had accused him of feeling guilty, and if you dealt in logic, that was the only solution she could think of.

A movement from the corner of her room startled her as Mark came toward her. He smiled down at her. "Try staying awake until I get through talking to you this time. Do you remember that Greg is here?"

Her eyes were wide open. "Yes, I remember. It was Thursday. What happened to the other days?"

Mark's smile didn't quite reach his eyes, and he held on to her hand that didn't have needles in it. "You tried out a little of everything: pneumonia, kidney infection, low blood—you name it."

Puzzled, she repeated, "Pneumonia? That's highly unlikely, isn't it, in this day and time?"

"Yes, very unlikely. Stacy, you've let yourself get run down, and I suspect you've been working some extra shifts when you need to be resting and being lazy for a change. Have you lost that appetite Colie is so proud of?"

She shook her head, and he asked, "Were you late going for your checkup after the miscarriage?"

"Yes."

He shook his head. "I'd have thought better of

you, Waring." He watched her as he asked, "Do you hurt anywhere?"

"My side hurts, and my head, not very much." Her lips parted in a smile but the green eyes were expressionless. Why was Greg still here? Hadn't he been due to leave on Sunday? She didn't ask the question, deciding he had probably run into a problem at the dormitory.

Mark was talking to her. "Boyd will be in with some bouillon for you, and I'll send in a capsule to help the pain." He stood up, still holding her hand. "Greg will be in to see you later. We weren't sure you'd be awake enough to talk tonight."

"What time of day is it?" She wanted to tell him she couldn't see Greg, but she would never be able to convince Mark.

"Five thirty in the afternoon. I have to go, but I'll see you on my late rounds, if you're awake. If not, then tomorrow." He bent, brushed his lips against her hair, and was gone.

The ceiling was white. She stared at it, because her head hurt too much to turn it. Greg was suffering his guilt in a big way now after she was so sick, and for not being able to find her in Alaska. Poor Greg. *What a mess I made of your life. You could be married to Greta and have a baby by now; one you didn't have forced on you. One of your choice, from one of your kind.* She swallowed the pain before it started and whipped her thoughts in another direction. Four days were blank behind her, but try as she would, she couldn't remember. Her last conscious thought was trying to decide if she should ask Greg to make love to her. *Wonder if I did? No, I would remember that, but maybe I asked, and he refused.*

"Hi, Stacy." Anna grinned at her. "Boy, am I glad you finally woke up. You scared us silly, you know." She set the small bowl of bouillon and crackers on Stacy's bed tray, and turned it so she could reach it. "Let me put you up some. Now, can you feed yourself?"

"Yes."

"Take this first." She fished a plastic case from her pocket, handed Stacy a pretty lavender and white capsule. "Dr. Grant sent that. And, speaking of Dr. Grant, he's been a worse bear than usual since you've been sick." Her voice lowered two decibels. "You know, Stacy, I think he was afraid you were gonna die."

Stacy laughed in spite of herself. "Oh, Anna. You're so dramatic. Of course, he didn't think I was dying."

An expression touched Anna's face for a second, and she looked away. "I don't know about that. You were mighty sick for a few days."

Stacy didn't ask any more questions, feeling she'd heard enough for one day. She concentrated on the soup. The heat felt good to her throat, but she couldn't finish even the small bowl.

"You can do better than that," Anna scolded.

"No, no more. Know what I'd really love to have?"

"What?"

"A strawberry soda. Doesn't that sound scrumptious?"

Anna grinned. "Not on my diet. For you, it might work." Her voice was dry. "I'll relay your wishes to Dr. Grant or Greg, either of whom think if you want the moon, we should wrap it for you."

"Calling my name in vain?" Greg was at the door, as Anna turned.

"Just telling Stacy how jealous I am of all the attention she's getting. See you later." She pulled the door almost closed behind her.

Stacy smiled at Greg with what she hoped was a passable one, her feelings carefully put away for the duration. Duration of what? Forever. Or until he left, whichever was sooner.

Greg was close, but he didn't touch her. "Is that all you can eat? I'll feed you."

"No, I don't want any more." She moved the tray aside, and he pushed it to the foot of the bed.

"You look a little better. Did Mark come by?" His eyes looked tired, and she guessed he was working hard on the dormitories.

"Yes." Her eyes took in the gray in his hair, the tightness around his mouth. She couldn't find the near-dimple from the angle he was holding his head.

"Stacy." He was standing, and now he picked up her left hand. "I have to leave tomorrow afternoon. I've already postponed it once." He rubbed her bare ring finger. "I'll be back in four weeks when I have the plans for the dormitories ready. I'd like to take you back with me."

She had a little discipline left. "No, Greg. It didn't work the first time; it wouldn't work now." She smiled at him, the green eyes telling him nothing.

"Stop feeling bad about how things turned out, go on and live your life the way you want to. I'm fine; no problems. Let me assure you, your guilt is unnecessary."

"Damn it, Stacy, I love you. I'm not on a guilt trip." He reached in his pocket and withdrew a tissue-wrapped object. "I've taken this everywhere I've been ever since you left, hoping I'd find you to return it." She looked at the sparkling circle of diamonds in his palm, then up at him.

Curiosity edged her voice. "Wasn't it enough to pay you back the money?"

"It's worth a little more than that." A glint of anger touched his eyes, sharpened his voice.

"That's what I thought."

"Stacy, listen."

"No, Greg, you listen. I'm not going back with you. Get a divorce on whatever grounds you need, and I'll sign it. You don't owe me anything, so there's no money or property involved, and you can make it plain and simple, with no contest from me."

He was quiet, watching her with his tired navy blue eyes, his mouth in a straight line. "Is that what you really want, Stacy? You're going to stay here with Mark?"

She didn't answer, but continued to watch him, her eyes recording all the features she loved. He stood there a long time, bent and kissed her, and said, "All right, Stacy," and walked away.

She was still lying there, wide eyed, when Mark came by. He checked her pulse. "You're looking awake, at least."

Stacy smiled. Yes, I'm awake, she wanted to say, but I wish I weren't. Panic had filled her as she had watched Greg walk out of the room away from her. All the soul-searching she had done as she lay in the hospital bed and all the conclusions she had reached had not helped her when it came time to say good-bye to him. She was starting over again with the same stark pain she had fought for over a year and she wasn't sure how much endurance was left in her.

"Are you going home with Greg when he finishes here?" He picked up her hand, rubbing the cold fingers.

"No. I told him to go ahead with the divorce."

"Stacy," Mark began, then stopped. "Are you sure it's what you want?"

All of a sudden everyone wants to know if it's what I want. Since when has that mattered? she wondered to herself. She smiled at Mark. "He thinks I'm staying because of you."

"And you let him?" Mark's voice was disapproving.

"It was his idea, not mine."

"You could have told him the truth. You know you're not in love with me, and he'll believe the worst."

She shrugged. "Does it matter, Mark? I told him once you were a good friend. Why do I have to keep saying it? Perhaps he wants to believe it to ease his own conscience." She was tired, and her eyes closed wearily.

"Do you want something to help you sleep?" he asked, sympathy for her in his voice.

She didn't open her eyes. "Yes. Forever."

"Stacy!" His voice came quick and sharp. "Don't you even think it." His hands caught her shoulders, shaking her. The green eyes with no expression opened wide, and she smiled a little. Her arms crept around his neck, and he held her close.

AS THE TIME neared for Greg's return Stacy grew more and more restless. After staying two weeks on the ranch with the entire Reynolds family looking after her, she moved, against all protests, back into a temporary room in the dormitory. The thought of Greg being back on the island, so close to her, sent her walking many nights along the beach, and she had no desire to have Kay and Don worrying about her. Mark promised her she could return to work within a week or ten days, but only thirty hours and all days; no night shifts for a few weeks. He knew nothing of her lonely walks on the beach or she would have heard from him by now.

She was sitting on her usual perch in Colie's kitchen, a glass of fresh pineapple juice in front of her. Colie watched her from the corner of his eye as he prepared the dishes for Mark's dinner party. Stacy no longer ate everything in sight, and even the juice was out of courtesy for Colie, he well knew. He had mentioned her lack of appetite to Mark the day before. "She eats nothing. No matter what I fix, she tastes, and that's all," he complained.

"Give her time, Colie. She was pretty sick," Mark tried to reassure him, but he too was worried. He knew only part of her problem was physical. Somehow, he knew Stacy still loved Greg, but her stubborn belief that he suffered only guilt kept her from accepting the fact that Greg spoke the truth when he told her he loved her. Maybe after Greg's absence from the island, she would have time to think it over, and believe him when he returned to finish his work at the dormitories.

Stacy sighed, drank the rest of the juice, and slid from the stool. "Thanks, Colie. See you later." He watched her from the kitchen window as she started up the street. At the corner she stopped and stood looking toward the park, turning finally in the direction of the beach, and out of his sight. He shook his head and returned to his work, but couldn't get the small figure out of his mind. He hadn't had the heart to tell her who one of Mark's special guests would be that night.

Stacy reached her favorite spot on the beach and dropped on the sand, staring across the blue-green Pacific. To her mind's eye came the picture of Greg's house, his monument to the desert, his mark of success. Success to Greg; home to her. It ever would be, no matter how far away she wandered. Hawaii was as lovely a place as she would ever find, but the lonely, wild desert fascinated her, perhaps because she too was wild and lonely.

It grew dark and Stacy stirred, with no desire to return to her room. Four walls to look at and only a twelve-by-twelve room to pace. Even her books held no interest for her.

As soon as he gets the divorce, I'm going to have me a fling, a real sex brawl, she vowed fiercely. Her body yearned for the touch of Greg's hands, remembering way back when, before she learned it was only she who loved. She straightened, put her shoulders back, and struck out on the run, but it didn't last long. Her breath gave out, and she had no strength for running. *I'm not worth a whole lot for anything,* she concluded in disgust.

She stood across the street from the dormitory Greg was remodeling. The only outward change was the west wall that had the sun deflectors on the roof and halfway down the side. The inner appearance was the beautiful part, and years ago she would have thought it heavenly to have a fifteen-by-fifteen private room with a built-in desk you could actually sit at. Built-in beds big enough for big women, much less someone Stacy's size. Apartment-size refrigerators and countertop stoves were in the kitchenettes of the efficiency apartments assigned to nurses who lived in the dorms full-time.

Stacy slept in the bed, but she seldom cooked anything. If she was empty before going to bed, she drank juice. If she was hungry, she went to see Colie. After all these years of looking out for herself, she had gotten around to taking the easy way out. Perhaps it was because she stayed tired so much of the time—or maybe it was pure laziness. Whatever, she grinned a little, thinking that she was beginning to enjoy doing nothing.

The hallways were still full of building materials and the closets in her room weren't quite complete, but she could tell the area would be the subject of many complimentary magazine and newspaper articles once Greg's work was completed. Whatever job he did, he did to perfection, even to breaking hearts, at which he was master. Disgusted with getting so close to self-pity, she threw herself across the bed and went to sleep.

Habit took her to the cafeteria the next morning where she sat off to herself with a cup of coffee that had grown cold. She looked up to see Greg moving toward her, and she stiffened as he approached her table.

"Hello, Stacy." He took in the tanned face, not quite as thin as three weeks before when he had last seen her. The green eyes still had dark shadows beneath them and held no readable expression.

"Greg. I wasn't expecting you for a week yet." She recognized the legal-size envelope in his hand and hoped the shiver that passed through her body wouldn't be noticed.

He didn't sit down, but placed the envelope on the table. "Here are the papers you wanted, Stacy. Look them over and let me know any changes you want made. I'll be here until Thursday." He walked away.

Her glance rested on the envelope, and she couldn't take her eyes away from it, fascinated by it as she would be by a rattler that suddenly appeared in front of her. There rested her past and future, and she had only the present to wrestle with. Her body broke out in a cold sweat and her scalp prickled, and she bit her lips as nausea threatened. Somehow she made it back to her room.

She didn't open the envelope till the afternoon, but left it where she could see it from her bed where she spent most of the day. She heard Anna leave for her shift at three, and got up, tucked the envelope under her arm, and headed for the beach. Low clouds scudded in over the high waves but Stacy paid no attention as she read through the legal brief, trying to reconcile the whereases, whyfores, hereafters, and parties of the first part to some meaningful language. Whatever the legal terms, they spelled the end to a marriage that never should have been. Gave Stacy back the right to use the name she had started life out with; gave Greg back his freedom; even put a name to Greg's albatross: irreconcilable differences.

She read on down the minute printing on the page, then reread it, certain some of it was a mistake. He was giving her the house and the car, free and clear.

You're crazy, Greg, she thought, tempted to throw the whole packet back in his face.

The first big splat of water brought her back to the present, and she looked up, realizing she was caught in a cloudburst, not uncommon to this part of the island of Hawaii. She didn't mind for herself, but, trying to protect the precious papers she carried, slipped them beneath her shirt, and took off at a run to Mark's, closer by a few blocks than the hospital. Drenched, she stopped beneath the carport, not wanting to step inside and risk ruining Colie's polished kitchen floor, but he had heard her and came out.

"Stacy! Get in here." Colie's face looked like the thunderclouds overhead. She had never seen him angry, but his dark eyes shot sparks at her. "Get out of those clothes and I'll get you something dry to put on."

"But, Colie—"

"Get!"

She got. Dripping down the hall to the bathroom, she laid the relatively dry papers on the floor, and stripped off her shirt and jeans, underclothes and all, then hung them over the shower bar after squeezing out the excess water.

"Here." Through the half-closed door, she accepted the terry robe from Colie that she had worn their first meeting.

She grinned and thought, *If Mark ever throws you away, I get dibs.* Snuggling into the wrap, she rolled the sleeves up over her hands, and taking the envelope with her, padded barefoot to the kitchen where Colie fumed to himself.

As he turned she put up her hands in defense. "Honest, Colie, I didn't notice the clouds till it was too late."

He eyed the still damp hair, clear green eyes, and a smile replaced the scowl. "I don't want you to be sick anymore, Stacy. I'm sorry I jumped at you."

Climbing on her favorite stool, she reached for the hot tea he had made. An aroma of tropic spices invaded her nostrils, and she took a long sip. "Delicious, Colie."

"Have you eaten today?"

"I don't believe so," she told him, trying to remember. She would now, or else, and she knew it, so made no protest when he placed a thick corned beef sandwich and a glass of milk in front of her.

She watched the rain coming down in a steady

Miracles Take Longer 227

downpour and surmised that it would last all night. It was already getting dark. "Mark on duty?"

"No. He and Mr. Fields left early to go to the ranch and were planning to stay all night." Colie looked around at her. "You can stay here and not go back out in the rain."

She gave in with no argument. "Thanks, Colie. I'm too tired to go six more blocks anyway." She ran a hand through her damp hair. "If it's okay with you, I'm ready for bed."

She lay awake in one of Mark's spare bedrooms, mulling over what to do with the divorce papers and changing her mind a dozen times. This was what she had waited over a year for, and here they were, handed to her, with a chance to return to her barren, fruitless desert, scene of happiness and heartbreak. The good, the bad, the indifferent. Phoenix Medical would probably hire her back, if Phyllis Dorn was still there. She sighed, turning restlessly. *Given my track record,* she decided, *whatever I do will be wrong.* She heard the door close behind Colie as he left, turned her head into the pillow, and cried herself to sleep, sobbing like a lost child.

Thursday morning, she went looking for Greg amid the debris and upheaval of the dorm remodeling. She found him involved in adjusting a complex lighting arrangement, so she stood back out of the way, taking in the total absorption he displayed in his work. Greg was one of the best at his job, never had complaints of sloppy work, and was able to take his pick of contracts. Some diabolical trick of fate had seen fit to have him select the Grant project and throw her world out of kilter once more. It had to happen.

He turned, rubbing his hand over his eyes, before he saw her. His glance took in the envelope in her hand, but he waited for her to speak.

"I signed the papers, Greg," she told him, without any other explanation. That was what he wanted, and that was what she was giving him, making one of them happy at least.

A quizzical smile touched his mouth for an instant and was gone. He looked down at her as she handed the papers to him. "No questions?"

She shook her head. "It's all very clear."

He eyed her for a moment, looked at the papers he held, shrugged, and said, "All right, Stacy."

She turned and left him looking after her. That night, as she lay awake in bed, a chill shook her so hard, the bed rocked. Greg was gone, the divorce papers signed, it would be final in six months, and reaction had set in. All that remained was to tell Mark her decision.

"You're what?" Mark's explosion wasn't unexpected.

"Greg's giving me the house and I'm going back to live in it."

"Waring—Stacy." He stopped, staring at her as if concluding she had at last taken leave of her senses.

She sat there, smiling at him, telling him without any expression whatsoever that she was leaving Hawaii, not going back to Greg, but back to his house.

"I can get things ready and try for the spring semester at the burn center in San Antonio. If I'm ever

Miracles Take Longer

going, now's the time. I've already called Phoenix Medical Center, and they'll take me back. I can stay in the dormitory there till the divorce is final." She wondered at her ability to talk about it without emotion. Unreal, that's what it was, unreal.

Mark took her to the ranch one last time to say good-bye to the Reynolds family. "We'll miss you, Stacy," Kay said. "If you change your mind about living in Arizona, come back and stay with us."

"I'll have a place for you to visit, and I want all of you to come to Phoenix. Will you?" Stacy asked. "You'll love the house."

"We've talked about going to the mainland for years, Stacy, and we want to see your house we've heard so much about it. I read Greg's book." Kay's smile was puzzled, and she hesitated over her next statement. "He does love you, Stacy, can't you tell?"

"I don't know, Kay. I think I'll be better off if I try to sort out things after I've been back on the mainland and at work for a while." She stood up. "Bring Colie with you when you come."

Kay laughed. "Try to keep him from going with us."

"I promise to cook for him instead of his having to cook for me. Bet he thinks I can't cook." She hugged Kay and the children and waved to Don as Mark opened the car door for her to get in. All the way back to Hilo, she sat huddled in the seat next to Mark, not wanting to talk. He understood, and at her dormitory he walked to the door with her, said good night, and left her alone with her thoughts.

The next morning Mark took her to the airport,

staying until her flight was called. "You've been quite an experience for me, and I wouldn't have missed it for the world," she told him, wanting to say more, but tears were close to the surface.

"Take care, Stacy. You still aren't strong enough to work as you did before, and it's important to pamper yourself now. Promise?" He smiled down at her as they called her flight number. "If you get through your school by next summer, let us know and we'll visit in the fall. According to Greg's book, that's a good time to visit Arizona."

"Yes, it is," she said, "And I'll be looking for you."

Finding her seat on the plane was difficult through the tears that kept falling.

Chapter Thirteen

Stacy waited a few minutes in the luxurious outer office of Talbert and Talbert, Attorneys at Law, eyeing the lovely, efficient secretary, thinking of Greta. When the inner office opened, she turned to meet the elder Talbert of the firm, Greg's lawyer whom she had never met.

"Mrs. Fields, please come in." Bernie Talbert was tall and straight, a head full of wavy hair the color of dull silver, blue eyes that looked directly at you, and a warm smile. "Greg told me you had signed the papers, but he hasn't brought them in yet. I had no idea you were in town."

She sat in the chair he indicated and asked, "He didn't bring them to you? Why?"

The lawyer looked at her. "Don't you know?"

She shook her head. "All I want is to let you know I'm in town and will be living in the dormitory at Phoenix Medical Center until the divorce is final."

"You can live in the house if you like. Greg gave me the keys with that stipulation." He smiled at her.

"He stays in the apartment and seldom goes to the house."

She shook her head again in confusion. "Why?"

He spread his hands. "Greg doesn't explain what he does to anyone. Right now he's in Tacoma for several days."

She made up her mind. "Fine. I'll take the keys, then. Is there anything else I should know about the provisions of the divorce?"

"I'll drop a copy of everything by the house tomorrow, if that's all right, Mrs. Fields." Mr. Talbert stood to escort her to the door, handing her a set of keys.

She looked at the keys in the outstretched hand, then around the well-appointed office, all beige, brown, and gold; the gold-lined diplomas and awards; a window that framed the fabulous Arizona sunsets. She smiled her good-bye and went out into the late fall sunlight.

Stacy didn't have the nerve to go to the house right away, and it was the next afternoon before she paid twenty-dollar cab fare to be taken out there. Along with the house key were the keys to her little green car.

"Wait," she told the driver and went to try the keys. The heavy door swung open for her as it had so many times before, and she waved the driver on, turning to watch as he drove away. Only then did she step back and look at the house. Miracle of the desert. *If this is Greg's miracle, what, then, am I? A prickly pear cactus in his side. I'm sorry, darling.*

Carrying the two pieces of new luggage inside, she put them down, closed the door, and locked it. Kick-

Miracles Take Longer

ing off her slippers, she took her time going from room to room. Mrs. Roper must still come and clean, she thought. Everything was spotless. The door to the nursery was closed and she stood a moment looking at Happy, the quilted dwarf, but she didn't touch it. She went on to the master bedroom and paused in the open door. The scene Star had painted was just where she had pictured it, reflecting the design of Greg's house in natural splendor. An odd image in the upper left corner seemed out of place and prompted her to walk closer.

Her breath caught as she leaned for a better look. For some unknown reason, Star had painted a miniature likeness of Stacy there, the green eyes laughing at the world, the heavy braids crowning her head, lips curved in a lilting smile. Fascinated, she stared. *The only time I ever felt like that was when Greg was loving me.*

Straightening, she glanced around the room. There had been no changes that she could tell. In the dressing room the mirror reflected a young woman with dark-circled green eyes, shoulder-length dark hair, swinging in a heavy wave back from bangs that curved over arrow thin brows. The pale yellow pantsuit outlined her slimness. She turned away, opened the big walk-in closet. The cashmere coat she had left still hung there with her maternity clothes and the wedding dress.

Retracing her steps, she turned down the hall to the kitchen. *I feel as if I belong here, but I'm not sure I do.* She opened the refrigerator; it was empty. She opened the big pantry door, seeing the well-stocked shelves, arranged in neat order. The double-lock slide bolt to the garage moved easily and the door swung wide to reveal her small green car sitting alone in the huge space. She walked to the back to see the up-to-date license plate that read: STACY.

Back in Greg's study, she stood near the bookshelves that lined the walls, filled with books on architecture and solar energy, many of which she had read or looked through. The scrapbook she had removed the picture from of Greg and Greta was in the same place. On his desk was a bound copy of his book, *Miracle of the Desert*. She picked it up, her fingers caressing the expensive leather cover, opening it automatically to the fly leaf. The familiar inscription in gold print stared back at her: TO STACY WITH LOVE—MIRACLES TAKE LONGER. She took it with her, curling up in the huge king-size bed, reading till she fell asleep.

Days of wonder for Stacy passed as she reexplored the desert surrounding the house. She stocked the refrigerator on the day she picked up the small trunk shipped air freight from Hilo, her first move with excess baggage that didn't fit into the blue cardboard case, finally discarded in favor of the pale gold luggage set she bought to return to the mainland. She didn't go back into Phoenix, having no desire to be there before she returned to work in two more weeks, and was content to rest and ramble. Remembering Mark's warning about her eating habits, she fixed at least one meal each day, drank milk and juices, taking the prescribed medicine and vitamins religiously. She often ate a big breakfast around noon, and fruit the rest of the day.

After I get back from the school, I'm gonna get a dog and a horse. Maybe Star will help me build a corral. Speaking of whom, guess I should go see them. In the baggage she had yet to unpack were gifts she had for Rachel, Star, and little Stacy Lee, but she was reluctant to leave the house. She stared across the shimmering desert from the mesa where she could see for miles, anything that moved north from Phoenix or that came down her lane, a half mile from the secluded house. There were few vehicles passing, and none came her way. That was fine; she sought no company. The only person she had seen was Bernie Talbert, who, true to his word, had brought a copy of the provisions of the divorce by. She had never opened them, and they lay on Greg's desk in his study in a place where she didn't go very much. Divorce was divorce, and she had no need for the gory details. The papers would wait.

She lay back on the hard rock, relaxing in the warm sunlight, closing her eyes and letting her mind glide in any direction it chose. It went back to Philadelphia, wondering about the woman who had found it necessary to abandon an unwanted little waif, wondering if the desperation were real or imagined; was it a selfish move or unselfish as far as her mother was concerned? Nothing would make her give up her child, she was positive, but she was different from—*I don't even know her name,* Stacy thought, her eyes opening wide to stare at the unblemished sapphire-blue of the desert sky. It had been a long time since she had even thought of the woman who gave birth to her, and any resentment she felt was long since gone. She could think of no reason why her mother had entered her thoughts, unless she associated her with Philadelphia. From Philadelphia, to Phoenix, to Alaska, to Hawaii, to Phoenix. *The circle is complete; I plan to stay right here, except for schools. The desert and the city, combined, will be big enough to hold both Greg and me since we don't move in the same circles.*

A faint hum forced its way into her consciousness and she frowned, hoping it would go away, finally sitting up to look for the offending sound. A car, and coming down her lane. She watched a moment, but didn't recognize the car, a small light-colored one, but not Bernie Talbert's nor Greg's pale blue one. *No one else knows I'm here. I could stay here and maybe they'll go away.* She sighed and rose to go. Anyone this far from the city was either lost or had a particular purpose in mind, so she ran lightly along the faint trail toward the house, pausing as she rounded the curve of the hill and the building came into her view. The car was parked in front of the garage.

By the time she reached the front yard, the driver of the car had disappeared and she hesitated, looking a moment at the unfamiliar car, shrugged, and started toward the back of the house. She rounded the corner and stopped, staring at the open door, and a chill hit her. She had never thought about being afraid, but how had that door opened?

I know I closed and locked it, she thought, frowning, uncertainty causing her to hesitate.

"Stacy?" The familiar voice kept her rooted to the spot as she watched Greg's tall figure emerge from the dim interior of the house. They stood, ten feet apart, staring at each other.

Greg spoke first. "Come in out of the sun, Stacy."

Willing her legs to move, she went past him, turning to look at him from across the breakfast bar where she had retreated.

Greg took in the slim figure in faded jeans and red T-shirt, jade-green eyes wide, pale rose-colored lips parted in surprise. "You've lost more weight." His voice was accusing.

Stacy swallowed. "I thought you were in Tacoma. And that isn't your car." It wasn't much of a statement, but it was all she could manage under the circumstances.

He grinned at her across the few feet that separated them; the old grin she remembered and loved. "I got home last night, and had a note from Bernie that you were here. I traded cars a few months ago." He watched her and when she said nothing, he asked, "Have you had breakfast?"

"No."

"Neither have I. Let's go into town and eat."

She had no desire to be in the car close to him, much less ride for miles sitting next to him. "Would you just as soon eat here? I have plenty of stuff to cook." Her voice came out normal, surprising her. Her insides were behaving any way but normal.

"All right," he agreed. "I'll help you."

They worked side by side in silence. She fried bacon as Greg set the table, poured orange juice, and put bread in the toaster, ready to be pushed down as soon as she put eggs in the pan, the same pattern they had followed many times when she was working and late getting home.

"The refrigerator was empty. When did you shop?" Greg was standing close behind her as he spoke.

She frowned, trying to remember what day it was, but they all ran together, and she gave up attempting to sort out the dates. "Whatever day I picked up my trunk; I can't remember. Two days ago, I think." She took up the bacon and beat the eggs to a golden texture, poured them into the buttered pan and stirred them gently. "Before you leave, let me give you what I brought Greta. I haven't unpacked anything yet, but maybe I can find it."

His voice was curious. "You brought something from Hawaii for Greta?"

"I thought she'd like one of the muumuus for lounging. It's in all shades of yellow and will be lovely with her coloring." She put the eggs in a bowl, smiling at him for the first time.

"Why?" He was very close, the bowl of scrambled eggs between them. "I thought you didn't like Greta."

Trembling at his closeness, she wet her lips. "I've always liked Greta." She looked down at the bowl she held, then up at him. "Just because I'm jealous of her doesn't mean I don't like her." She moved around him to place the eggs on the table.

His hands on her arms turned her to face him. "Why are you jealous of Greta, who happens to be happily married to Stubbs?"

She tried to pull away, not fully comprehending what he said, intent only in keeping him from knowing what he was doing to her. "She's so pretty, and efficient, and always with you. It's natural that I'd be jealous."

"Greta and I have been friends since grade school, and I was best man at her wedding." He tilted her chin, forcing her to look at him. Her eyes widened, and he read panic there, uncertainty at what he planned to do.

"Are you afraid of me, Stacy?" he asked. A sudden picture of a proud young woman telling him she always paid her debts came before him, and he smiled down at her. Two years ago? Stacy would be twenty-nine years old, and she was still so young, but perhaps she would always be. He pulled her against him, letting her realize he needed her, wanting her to know he belonged to her in every way. One hand slid behind her hips, holding her immovable as he pressed his hard body into hers; the other fingered the gold chain at her neck. "You're still wearing the chain I gave you our first Christmas together," he whispered.

Stacy looked up into his eyes. "I've never taken it off, Greg. All this time."

"I want to kiss you, Stacy." As she made a move to withdraw from him, his arms tightened. "And whether you give me permission or not, I intend to do just that."

Smoky green eyes stared up at him, into the smoldering navy blue eyes, determined mouth close to hers. "The eggs will get cold."

"To hell with the eggs." His head bent to hers.

"Please, Greg, don't." It was only a whisper, which he had no intention of hearing.

"Stacy." His low voice crooned her name as his hands caressed her stiff body, going upward from her hips to fasten in the shining dark hair growing longer to her shoulders now. His free hand slid from her arm to her waist, using his fingers to hook into her belt, forcing her up off her feet so she had no way to brace away from him. His mouth touched hers, and the tremor through her body brought a moan from Greg as he realized her lips had parted for his. Plundering gently, the tip of his tongue forced her teeth apart, the pressure pushing her head back into the palm of his hand.

She leaned against him, her hand moving from protest on his chest to circle behind his head, tangling in the crisp dark hair to hold his mouth to hers. All the months of denial went into her kiss as she moved her body closer, Greg's hand left her belt to slip upward to her shoulder to her breast, caressing the firm mound, back down to her waist, doubling his hold on her slender hips, straining her against him. A groan escaped him as he lifted his head, looking down at the dark lashes fanned over her cheeks. The lashes moved, swung upward to reveal dreamy green eyes, questioning the removal of his mouth from hers. He lifted her, and a few easy strides took them to the bedroom, where he laid her on the gold spread. She stared up at him, seeing the intent in his eyes.

"If you do, the divorce papers will be null and void," she reminded him.

His mouth lingered on her before he said, "I know." Her belt buckle came undone with a click; the zipper responded to his agile fingers; his hands in-

Miracles Take Longer 241

vaded her body beneath the red T-shirt, finding the catch to her bra, which offered little resistance to him. His mouth rested lightly on hers, his exploring hands, finding bare firm flesh, became gentle in their manipulation, caressing the nipples growing hard in his fingers. Lifting her shoulders, he pulled the shirt off, the bra going with it, as his head lowered to put his mouth against the hollow of her throat, just before moving to the hard brown tip of her breast, which his hand released to his warm, searching lips. She drew a shuddering breath, holding his head immovable for an instant, then pulled him away.

"Greg."

His voice thick with his desire for her, he said, "Don't tell me to stop, Stacy, because you know I can't." A tiny smile curved his mouth as his eyes devoured her face, the warm moist lips, the rumpled dark hair shining over the gold of the spread.

"I don't want you to stop, but—" She ran the tip of her tongue over her lips, watching him uncertainly.

At her hesitation he kissed her parted lips and prompted, "But?"

"I don't know how to say this, Greg, except—" She touched his mouth and her words tumbled out. "It will be like the first time for me, or almost that way."

It was a moment before realization reached him, and his hands resting on her bare shoulders tightened. "I don't understand."

She closed her eyes, then opened them wide to watch him. "When a woman has a baby, she naturally becomes tighter afterward. Until she resumes sexual activity." The rest of her speech was a whisper. "I haven't."

The navy blue eyes shadowed as he looked down at her. "The miscarriage?"

Her voice barely audible, she said, "Yes."

"Darling," he whispered. "Oh, sweetheart." He turned the spread back, picked her up, and placed her on the cool sheets. Without a word he removed her jeans, then her panties, and she lay naked before him.

"Do you want me to hold you first?" he asked, his words as gentle as his hands.

She sighed. "Yes."

He lay beside her, pulling her up to lie on his shoulder, cuddling her, his hands beginning a gentle massage over her hips and thighs.

The months of separation vanished as she watched him through half-closed eyes, and a shiver shook her body as she pressed herself to him. His lips parted slightly, showing just the edge of his teeth, and she put her fingers to his mouth, feeling his warm breath on them. Her forefinger pushed between his lips and teeth, and he bit gently into her flesh. Her mouth tilted in the ghost of a smile, the tip of her tongue touching the corner. Greg's hand came up to push the heavy bangs away from her eyes, sweeping the dark waves back over her ear, one finger tracing the cheekbone to her chin, taking her finger from his mouth, his lips drifting down to hers. He held her fingers against his throat where the pulse hammered as his desire for her went beyond his control.

"Sweetheart?" He drew a ragged breath and his arm tightened, then slowly let her go, pushing her against the pillow, his eyes going over her completely, taking in the slim body that belonged to him, before he leaned toward her again.

She lay, only half awake, as Greg's hands and lips caressed her body, realizing she had never forgotten the feelings he always aroused in her. Each nerve in her body responded separately to his touch, and she was suddenly wide awake as he trailed kisses from her throbbing breasts down across her flat belly, conscious of the liquid fire coursing through her, as she gasped, turning to him, begging for fulfillment. The domed ceiling exploded in a galaxy of northern lights, the cascading sweetness almost a pain as her body writhed beneath his lovemaking.

"Stacy." There was no yesterday or tomorrow, only now, as Greg claimed her for his own, his husky whisper telling her what she needed to hear. Bodies wrapped together, they lay quiet a long time.

It was he who finally broke the silence. "I didn't file the divorce papers, baby."

She didn't move, but asked her question against his throat. "Why?"

"I never intended to give you up. Never." His arms were tight around her slim body. "I was thirty-two years old before I found you. You were mine for just a little while, and I lost you, because I didn't have sense to know you were all I would ever need or want. We could never have made such a bargain if we hadn't known, deep down, that it was for keeps. Now that I've got you back, nothing will make me give you up." He looked down into her sleepy eyes. "Unless you don't love me."

"I love you, Greg. All I ever wanted was your happiness." She let her hand slip from his ribcage to stroke his narrow hips.

"You are my happiness, Stacy. Do you need a memory course to keep that in mind?"

Smiling, she pulled him to her, lying still for a few seconds, then letting her hands explore his body, delighting in the rediscovery that she could bring him to her so quickly in complete surrender.

As their bodies blended into one he whispered the words she needed to hear above all, "I love you, Stacy."

It was a long time later that he asked, "Wonder if our eggs are still warm."

She turned to him and they burst out laughing. Looking past him, she spotted the odd inset on the picture.

She pointed. "Why did Star do that?"

Greg kissed her finger pointed at the painting. "I told him I didn't have any pictures of you and since the house was yours, you should be in the picture." He stared at the painting and his voice held wonder. "Isn't it odd that Star knew exactly the way I remembered you? He couldn't have been more accurate if you had been standing there."

"Flatterer." She smiled at him in lazy satisfaction. "Greta's married?"

The sudden question came unbidden, and she stared at him. She had heard him, but too many things had happened, and she had pushed it into the inner recesses of her mind.

"Uh-huh. Last Christmas. She and Stubbs became

engaged just after you left." Greg's eyes were hidden behind half-closed lids, as he looked down at her, and she could feel hurt in him. "I'm sorry you were jealous of her. There was no need."

"Mark?"

He grinned at her. "Okay, you win. No jealousy on either side. All right?"

"All right." She rolled back into his arms, her voice soft. "I'm tired, Greg. Hold me."

Stacy's breath was uneven against his throat as her body, still tense, lay in his arms. Her hand, lying on his waist, made restless movements over his ribcage, fingers outlining each rib separately, and she rubbed her cheek into the curled chest hair. One knee was drawn up across his legs, and he let his hand slide slowly over her hips, to the inside of her thigh, probing into the firm flesh. He massaged with slow, gentle caresses until her body jerked convulsively and she turned onto her back, her eyes wide green pools of brightness. The tip of her tongue touched the corner of her mouth, moving over her lips, leaving them moist and parted as he lowered his face to hers. Their warm breaths mingled as he hesitated, until she made an indistinguishable sound that he recognized as begging for his touch. The tender kiss became bruisingly insistent as her arms gathered him to her, giving herself to him with an urgency equaled only by the need in him. She cried out and his name was all he heard, all he needed to hear.

"You're home to stay forever, darling," he whispered.

He held her until the slender, naked body relaxed

against him, and her even breathing told him she was asleep. She sighed as he moved away, pulling the tangled sheet up to cover her. He stood looking down at her still form, not quite believing that she was back where she belonged, and he would never let her out of his sight for very long anymore.

Reluctantly he left her alone in the big bed, letting her sleep for an hour before he awakened her to eat.

"Do you want breakfast in bed, lazy bones?" Greg asked, bending to kiss the sleep-curved mouth.

Half-open eyes regarded him, and slender arms wrapped around his neck. "Before or after I have you?"

"Don't tempt me. We've already ruined one breakfast, and at the price of food, we can't afford to throw out another one."

"You sure?" She had no idea how hard it was to say no to her.

A fierce thrill of possessiveness went through him. "You have five minutes for a very quick shower, lover." He patted her sheet-covered hip and went out of the room.

GRETA WATCHED Greg prowl restlessly in his office, wondering a little at his obvious preoccupation with something other than the plans spread on his desk. Unusual in itself, because he worked hard and enjoyed it. Stacy had been back ten months, and seeing them together, she was happy for them, remembering how lost Greg had been without her, even though he never mentioned their troubles to anyone that she knew about. She had watched unhappiness settle on him like a heavy coat, but friend that she was, she hadn't been able to help him. Working eighteen hours a day, he had pushed himself as never before and looked as though he hadn't rested the other six hours left in the day. But, whatever had happened, he had kept it between Stacy and himself.

She looked up as he stopped in front of her desk. "I'll be at home, Greta. If Stubbs gets back before I do, call me."

She watched him leave, smiling. The restless movements didn't mean he was unhappy; on the contrary. He only needed to be with Stacy.

Greg drove straight home, taking in the award-winning desert landscaping of the yard as he parked outside the garage. He unlocked the front door and stood in the cool silence; the house was pleasant, even in August, without air-conditioning.

He frowned, listening. "Stacy?" Her car was in the garage so she had to be close by even if she wasn't expecting him to come home at this time of day.

He went down the hallway to the open door of their bedroom and paused. Stacy lay on her stomach on his side of the bed, dark hair splayed over his pillow, her face turned away from him.

'Stacy?"

She rolled over to smile sleepily up at him. The sheet dropped away from her, exposing bare shoulders and the beginning swell of her breasts.

"Are you sick?" He knelt beside her.

"No. I was waiting for you." Her voice was soft, her words slow.

"Did I tell you I'd be home?" He was trying to remember.

"No, but I knew you would."

"Oh?"

"Uh-huh. I need you."

She lifted her arms and he sat beside her, watching with interest as the sheet slid further down her body. Their lips met, and his mouth teased hers until she trembled and drew in her breath. With gentle hands he supported her breasts, moving back to look into her eyes, usually wide open, now sleepy-looking, long lashes making shadows across them. Her hands came away from his shoulders, stopping at the top button of his shirt. Undoing all the buttons, she pushed the shirt away, her hands going beneath the V-neck opening of his T-shirt over his ribcage, up to the hard muscled shoulders, her eyes following the movement of her hands. Her fingers probed down his back to the narrow waist and back again to link behind his head.

"Stacy." His voice drew her eyes back to meet his, searching for an answer to her need.

Her mouth curved. "Do you love me, Greg?"

"More than I could ever tell you."

"Show me." It was a soft command. She moved over without releasing her hold on him, giving him enough room to stretch his long body beside her, pressing into him as he complied with her request.

She had given him an easy task, for Stacy was easy to love. Her cool skin was satin-soft to his fingers, her body pliant to his touch. Her slimness molded itself to his hard muscled frame, not allowing him to pull away even had he wanted to. He heard the soft whisper of her breath as it came more quickly, felt her body tense beneath his exploring hands. Her mouth came against his, her lips moist, demanding, yielding in turn, and he squeezed his eyes shut as her hands urged him into her softness, the pulsing release bringing forth their twin moans of unbelievable sweetness.

As she lay close in his arms, his thumb caressed her lips, feeling her warm breath coming evenly. She stirred and murmured, "Do you mind if we name him Mark Bryan?"

He moved his head back to look down into her face. "What?"

"We're going to have a baby." She smiled, watching him. "Your mouth's open, darling."

"How long have you known?" he demanded.

"About ten minutes."

He sat up straight, dumping her unceremoniously on the pillow. "All right, Stacy, explain."

She gazed innocently up at him. "That's all there is to it. I'm pregnant. Just now."

"You can't know that." He watched her with narrowed eyes, doubting what he had heard, knowing somehow that she would convince him if she set her mind to it.

"Bet?"

"Stacy, you'll drive me crazy. Tell me what you're talking about. Right now." He could make his demands, but she had him where she wanted him, and they both knew it.

"I can go for a quick test, or we can wait the usual

six weeks, or you can take my word for it, darling. But I'm pregnant," she said, still smiling at him.

He considered her statement again and made up his mind. "You were already pregnant and just hadn't told me."

"No. He'll be born in May."

"And you're sure it will be a boy?" His voice was soft now, believing her.

"Yes." Her hand went up to touch his eyes, to his mouth, where he made a kiss against her fingers, to the suggestion of a dimple in his chin. "A little boy with navy blue eyes and almost a dimple right there."

"Will you be all right?" he asked, long fingers smoothing the damp bangs from her forehead. "Are you sure we should?"

"Everything will be fine. Don't worry. And it's a little late to ask if we should." Her smile convinced him.

He leaned to brush his lips against her hair, to her temple, down her cheek, nibbling at her parted lips. His hand drifted over her shoulder, touching the firm mound of her breasts, across the firm flatness of her stomach. He leaned back to regard her with solemn eyes. "Tell you what. If you're right I'll buy you that diamond pendant we looked at the other day."

She shook her head. "I don't want jewelry."

"You'll need a new car."

"No."

"What then? We are going to celebrate, aren't we?"

Her hands framed his face. "If I'm right, then eighteen months later, we'll have Heidi Janette."

He shook his head. "You're impossible, but you know what? I think I believe you. You have finally driven me crazy."

She laughed, pulling him down to her. "Shall we make doubly sure that I'm right?"

Readers rave about Harlequin American Romance!

"...the best series of modern romances I have read...great, exciting, stupendous, wonderful."
—S.E., Coweta, Oklahoma

"...they are absolutely fantastic...going to be a smash hit and hard to keep on the bookshelves."
—P.D., Easton, Pennsylvania

"The American line is great. I've enjoyed every one I've read so far."
—W.M.K., Lansing, Illinois

"...the best stories I have read in a long time."
—R.H., Northport, New York

"The stories are great from beginning to end."
—M.W., Tampa, Florida

"...excellent new series...I am greatly impressed."
—M.B., El Dorado, Arkansas

"I am delighted with them...can't put them down."
—P.D.V., Mattituck, New York

"Thank you for the excitement, love and adventure your books add to my life. They are definitely the best on the market."
—J.W., Campbellsville, Kentucky

*Names available on request.

◆ Harlequin

35 years of publishing the very best in romance fiction, beautiful contemporary novels by world-famous authors.

Reviewers across the country know that Harlequin is No. 1...

"When it comes to romantic novels... Harlequin is the indisputable king."
— *New York Times*

"The most popular reading matter of American women today."
— *Detroit News*

"Nothing quite like it has happened since *Gone with the Wind*."
— *Los Angeles Times*

Harlequin Books
The most popular love stories in the world!

Wherever paperback books are sold, or through Harlequin Reader Service.

In the U.S.
1440 South Priest Drive
Tempe, AZ 85281

In Canada
649 Ontario Street
Stratford, Ontario N5A 6W2

HAR-GEN-1

BOOK MATE PLUS®

The perfect companion for all larger books! Use it to hold open cookbooks... or while reading in bed or tub. Books stay open flat, or prop upright on an easellike base... pages turn without removing see-through strap. And pockets for notes and pads let it double as a handy portfolio!

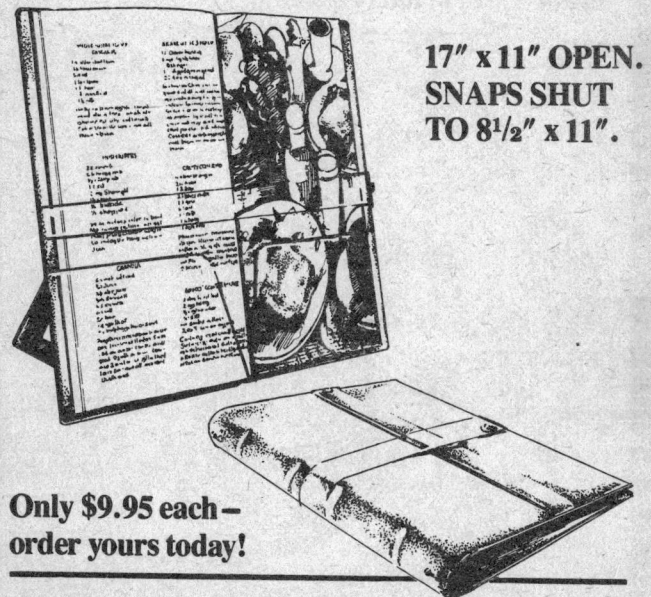

17" x 11" OPEN. SNAPS SHUT TO 8½" x 11".

Only $9.95 each – order yours today!

Available now. Send your name, address, and zip or postal code, along with a check or money order for just $9.95, plus 75¢ for postage and handling, for a total of $10.70 (New York & Arizona residents add appropriate sales tax) payable to Harlequin Reader Service to:

Harlequin Reader Service

In U.S.
P.O. Box 52040
Phoenix, AZ 85072-9988

In Canada
649 Ontario Street
Stratford, Ont. N5A 6W2

Introducing...

Harlequin American Romance

An exciting new series of sensuous and emotional love stories—contemporary, engrossing and uniquely American. Long, satisfying novels of conflict and challenge, stories of modern men and women dealing with life and love in today's changing world.

Available wherever paperback books are sold, or through Harlequin Reader Service:

In the U.S.
1440 South Priest Drive
Tempe, AZ 85281

In Canada
649 Ontario Street
Stratford, Ontario N5A 6W2

AR-5